IT WAS NOW OR NEVER!

As the chauffeur switched on the ignition and pulled away from the curb, Dani ran up to the limousine and hurled herself in, landing on a very surprised Clint MacPherson.

"Oh, God!" the chauffeur cried. "Does she have a gun?"

What Clint saw before him was a tangle of arms and shapely legs coming out from beneath a Western outfit. A flurry of long blond hair seemed to be everywhere. The eyes that looked up at him with a mixture of bravado and chagrin were blue. Sky blue. Soul-melting blue. Unless he was grossly mistaken, this woman did not have the makings of a kidnapper. But there *was* something about her. . . .

Dear Reader,

Welcome to Silhouette! Our goal is to give you hours of unbeatable reading pleasure, and we hope you'll enjoy each month's six new Silhouette Desires. These sensual, provocative love stories are both believable and compelling—sometimes they're poignant, sometimes humorous, but always enjoyable.

Indulge yourself. Experience all the passion and excitement of falling in love along with our heroine as she meets the irresistible man of her dreams and together they overcome all obstacles in the path to a happy ending.

If this is your first Desire, I hope it'll be the first of many. If you're already a Silhouette Desire reader, thanks for your support! Look for some of your favorite authors in the coming months: Stephanie James, Diana Palmer, Dixie Browning, Ann Major and Doreen Owens Malek, to name just a few.

Happy reading!

Isabel Swift
Senior Editor

SDRL-7/85

MARIE NICOLE
Country Blue

Silhouette Desire

Published by Silhouette Books New York

America's Publisher of Contemporary Romance

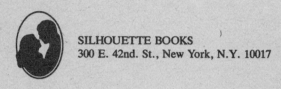

SILHOUETTE BOOKS
300 E. 42nd. St., New York, N.Y. 10017

Copyright © 1985 by Marie Rydzynsky

Distributed by Pocket Books

ISBN: 0-373-05224-3

First Silhouette Books printing August, 1985

10 9 8 7 6 5 4 3 2 1

MARIE NICOLE is a natural romance writer because her own life has been so romantic. She met her husband in tenth grade and began dating him in college. The first time he kissed her he made the room fade away, and things have only gotten better for them since.

To Evey Wolff-Ebert,
who hated
John Wayne movies
as much as I
loved them.

1

Dani Christopher wasn't used to stalking men, even men as handsome as Clint MacPherson. But then, Dani wasn't used to waking up in her motel room to find her van, her money and her so-called manager gone, either. Desperate times bred desperate measures, and if there was anything that Dani was right at this moment, it was desperate. Also mad.

Not at her "prey." She didn't even know him. She was mad at life in general for having dealt her this hand, and at Jared Kendall in particular for having taken both her affection and her money and run out on her without so much as a backward glance or a note. She hadn't even had the satisfaction of having something to tear up. She would have preferred to take her wrath out on Jared, but she would have settled for a note. She had been cheated on all counts.

Most people, she had told herself as she sat in her airless motel room, trying to pull her thoughts together, would have called it quits and gone home. Or wired for bus fare home, as the case was. But most people weren't as headstrong as Dani. Most people hadn't dreamed of being a singer all their lives.

"This way, Mr. MacPherson."

Dani came alive as she heard the words. A chauffeur was waving Clint MacPherson over to a limousine. A chauffeur! Dani bit her lip. This wasn't going to be easy at all. She had already been turned away at Clint's office by a crisp, cold secretary who had informed her that she couldn't see Mr. MacPherson without an appointment, and that his appointment book was filled up six months in advance.

Dani didn't want to wait six months. She didn't even want to wait six minutes. But she had. She had waited a lot longer than six minutes, in fact, standing in the doorway of an adjacent office building, her glazed eyes coming alive each time she saw someone emerge from the Tyson Building. If this hadn't been San Francisco, she knew she would have attracted a lot more stares than she did. But all sorts of outfits were "in" in San Francisco, so her fringed jacket, cowboy hat and spangled western dress didn't garner more than a casual glance from most passersby.

Her legs had begun to ache, and she had felt herself growing stiff. Was he going to stay in the building forever? She had absolutely no idea when Clint MacPherson planned to leave, and only a vague idea of what he looked like, thanks to a profile shot she had spotted on the wall of his office before his bulldog of a secretary had ushered her out. All Dani knew was that Clint was probably her last hope.

If Jared, the rat, hadn't taken her VW van, Dani could have tried a less flamboyant approach. She could have followed Clint to his house or apartment, or whatever he lived in, and tried to appeal to his sympathies there. But she was without any means of transportation. That left her only one avenue of approach.

As the chauffeur switched on the ignition and pulled away from the curb, Dani ran up to the slowly moving limousine, threw open the door and hurled herself in, landing on a very surprised Clint MacPherson.

"Oh, God!" the chauffeur cried, alarmed. "Does she have a gun?"

What Clint MacPherson saw before him was a tangle of arms and shapely legs coming out from beneath a Western outfit. A flurry of long blond hair seemed to be everywhere. The eyes that looked up at him with a mixture of bravado and chagrin were blue. Sky blue. Soul-melting blue. Unless he was grossly mistaken, this woman did not have the makings of a kidnapper.

"No, Fred," Clint said, "she's not armed. But I think Belle Starr here has us confused with someone else."

Dani pulled herself off his lap, trying to gather her dignity despite the absurdity of the situation. "No, I don't," she corrected him. "It's you I want."

"God, not another one," she heard the man called Fred mutter under his breath as he turned his attention back to the city streets.

"I'm highly flattered, Miss, um . . . ?" Clint raised an eyebrow in her direction, waiting.

"Dani Christopher," Dani said quickly, sitting on the edge of the leather seat as she turned to face him. "And I . . ." Dani's voice trailed off as she felt the car slowing down again. Why were they stopping?

"Want me to let her out on the corner?" Fred asked.

Now that he had established that Dani wasn't trying to kidnap Clint, the chauffeur took a rather condescending tone as he referred to Dani.

"Oh, no, please don't!" Dani cried, grabbing hold of Clint's lapels.

With firm hands, Clint tried to loosen her fingers. It required more strength than he had expected. The woman has some grip, he thought. "Perhaps there's someplace you'd like us to drop you?" he suggested, hoping that that would be the end of it. He had spent a long day tied to his phone, fighting for percentage points, arranging the best deals for his clients, and he was in no mood for an eccentric-looking woman in fringes, no matter how appealing.

"Your house," Dani answered.

Oh. She was one of those. Willing to trade anything for a shot at stardom. Clint shook his dark head slowly. "Thank you for the offer, but I'm afraid—"

Dani suddenly realized just what it was he thought she was offering. She tried not to sound indignant as she continued talking. "All I'm offering to do is sing for you."

By the look on Clint's face, she knew she was in grave danger of losing his attention. "Look," she cried, her fingers back on his lapels, this time holding on for dear life. She made him look her directly in the eyes. "Why don't you listen to me? I'm good." How weak and unconvincing those words must sound to him. Not to mention overused, she thought in desperation.

"I'm sure you are," Clint began mechanically, having been through this more times than he cared to think about. "But—"

"There is no 'but,'" Dani told him. "I've got a good, clear, clean voice, and all I want to do is sing."

"And get rich," Clint added with a touch of sarcasm born of the business he had been in for ten years.

Dani squared her shoulders. She didn't like what he was saying, but she forced herself to bite back her angry words. She had to make him understand and help her. "If that happens, terrific. But I won't die if it doesn't. I just want to earn my living singing. Why are all you agents too busy to even listen?" she demanded, her desperation escaping into her voice.

"Shall I head toward the police station?" Fred asked, having kept an ear on the conversation.

Dani's heart hammered in her ears as she looked from the back of Fred's black-capped head to the expression on Clint's face. She didn't see the strong jawline, the almost classic features that made up his handsome face, or the sensuous mouth that was given to easy smiles. All Dani saw was that the man on whom she had pinned all her fading hopes was about to have her thrown out of his car.

Ever since she had embarked on her singing career, leaving behind a bevy of well-wishers in the small Idaho town that had held her prisoner for twenty-five years, she had known nothing but travail and hard knocks. Jared's disappearing act after she had trusted him so implicitly had been the icing on the cake. Encased in numbing shock, Dani had found herself flipping through the pages of a public telephone booth's yellow pages. Clint's name had leaped out at her. It was the only one she had recognized under the listing of theatrical agents. She had read enough in the trade papers to come across his name time and again. He was the top. He only handled the very best.

He would laugh in her face.

But what did she have to lose? she had argued with

herself as she tore out the page and tucked it into her purse. Maybe the man was long overdue for a good deed. Maybe she could be it. It had been the only thought that sustained her while she hitchhiked across town to Clint's offices.

Dani had been full of the hyped bravado that desperation brings. It had helped her brave the critical, condescending glare that she had received from Clint's secretary, and had seen her through the time she spent standing in the building's doorway, waiting for him. But now her bravado was just about spent, eroded by a series of events that would have sapped the strength of a less determined individual. For almost a year now, she had been appearing in one unimpressive honky-tonk after another. Country and western music was bigger than ever, and there had been no shortage of clubs— "saloons" as they billed themselves—for Jared to book her in to. But they all had the same dreary effect on her, and she seemed to have the same unimpressive effect on them. People weren't listening, and her career just wasn't taking off. This wasn't the way the dream was supposed to turn out.

Despite everything, Dani believed in herself, believed that if she could perform in a place where the people were more interested in listening than in hurling witticisms at her or out-shouting each other, she would attain the success she dreamed she was destined for.

But even blind faith had to bow to overwhelming evidence at some point, and as Dani had sat in her motel room that morning she had told herself that if she couldn't get an agent to listen to her and agree to represent her, she'd give up. The prospect of taking her place amid the community in American Falls, Idaho, the way her family had always insisted she do, filled her with a cold, clammy dread. That dread was what spurred her on now.

Dani wasn't about to get out of the car until she had Clint's word that he'd listen to her sing.

"You drop me off at the police station," Dani said, brazening the situation out, "and you'll be missing the chance to handle the biggest star who ever walked into your office."

"Humph." Fred had responded to her words before Clint had a chance to.

Clint allowed himself a smile. And where had he heard that before? During his career as an agent with the topflight MacPherson-Reynolds Agency, he had heard those exact words countless times. Having been assaulted by the pleading words of would-be stars on a regular basis, there wasn't a reason in the world why he shouldn't take Fred up on his suggestion and get rid of this outlandishly dressed woman by scaring her with the threat of an arrest.

And yet, he didn't.

On the surface, she didn't look as if she'd be frightened that easily. But Clint thought he could detect a hint of fear in her eyes. Veiled, but there. He was too good an agent not to see it. Clint studied her while pretending not to. He was good at that, he thought in self-congratulation, having learned the trick from his father. His father had been the original MacPherson of MacPherson-Reynolds and had passed on not only the agency to his son, but also his knack for instinctively discerning talent. In the firm's thirty-eight-year history, it had backed very few also-rans. And when it had, it had usually been Reynolds who had picked them.

Sleek, good lines, Clint thought, even under those crazy fringes. A warm, sensuous mouth, and eyes that could melt a snowdrift in subzero weather. Not a bad combination for a performer, he judged. But what was he thinking of? His client file was filled to overflowing. His personal life was next to nonexistent. The only women he saw were the ones who trooped through his office, or called him at three in the morning, needing to have their hands held while they went through a sudden anxiety attack. Or the women who hurled themselves into his moving car. He had to admit that that was a rather novel approach.

He was smiling at her. Ever so faintly, but it was a smile. Dani took heart.

"No, I don't think we'll go to the police station just yet, Fred," Clint said without turning toward the driver. He thought he heard Fred mutter something under his breath. Like the business, Clint had inherited Fred from his father. Fred lived at the house and seemed to allow his life to revolve around Clint's clientele and the world of show business in general. He tended to grumble a lot. Clint would have worried if he didn't.

Clint made himself comfortable in the lushly uphol-stered limousine. "All right, Belle Starr, tell me why I should take you on." He arched an inquisitive brow in her direction as he waited for her response.

"Because I'm good," she said.

"You'll have to do better than that," Clint told her. "I have a full load of clients, all of whom are *very* good."

Dani didn't like the vulnerable position she was in. She was literally baring her soul to a total stranger, putting her heart on the line. But there wasn't any other choice.

"Because I thought that maybe you were fresh out of good deeds in your high-gloss world and needed one to feel good about." Dani wet her lips, not realizing how very appealing she looked at that moment. The afternoon sun penetrated the tinted windows and filtered through her golden hair, giving it an ethereal quality. "I need you," she added honestly.

Clint had been subjected to pleas before. Many. Some had grated on his nerves. Some had made him feel bad when he turned them down. This one, though, was different, and he tried to analyze what it was that made it so. He realized it was the woman. She looked more like a half woman, half waif, both terribly attractive, even in the clothes she was wearing. He could see Albert Reynolds giving him that pinched frown of his as he peered over his rimless glasses, his little eyes like two black marbles lost in pools of white water. Albert was semiretired and loved to lecture him on the evils of overdoing.

"All right," Clint agreed. "I'll listen to you."

Relief, joy and euphoria all flooded through Dani, crowding each other in quick succession. Before she knew what she was doing, she had thrown her arms around Clint's neck and hugged him. It was purely a reflexive action, born of innocence. But it didn't end up that way. The kiss she had aimed at his cheek landed by some riotous quirk of fate on his lips as he turned his head in surprise. The kiss that followed startled them both in different ways. Clint, his father had always said proudly, was never one to let an opportunity slip through his fingers. Or, in this case, his lips. Finding Dani's lips against his, he did what came naturally and accepted the offered gift.

Dani, nonplused, found herself on the receiving end of the warmest, most overwhelmingly delicious kiss she had ever experienced. This certainly hadn't been on her mind when she had impulsively thrown her arms around him. But it was nice. Very nice. As a matter of fact, it was the nicest thing that had happened to her in a long, long time. It was the kind of kiss, she couldn't help thinking, that poems were written about in the days when people were still writing poems to one another. It was the kind of kiss that knocked every single thing out of your head, including your name, your address and your life's ambition.

It was the kind of kiss, Dani thought in deepest sorrow, that should have come from a lover, not an agent.

Dani ended it first, albeit with a spark of reluctance. "I'm . . . I'm sorry," she stammered, flustered. She was experiencing the kind of feeling you have when you suddenly look down and realize that you are wearing two completely different shoes. "I don't know what happened. I didn't mean for it—"

Halt, her mind cried. Keep stammering like that and he's going to think you're some simpering ingenue who just fell off the potato truck.

But if she didn't say *something,* he was going to think that she was trying to buy him with promised favors, and that was the *last* thing she wanted him to think. She fully intended to make it on talent alone.

Dani cleared her throat, her voice dropping two octaves. "You shifted your head," she said with a touch of accusation in her voice, putting the blame for the kiss squarely on his shoulders.

He wore the blame well. Clint grinned, and she found that his smile served to render an already exquisitely handsome face even more appealing. Agents weren't supposed to be handsome, she thought, only masterful.

"Lucky me," he murmured.

16

The sound of his lowered voice did something to her. It struck a nerve which rippled down to the base of her spine, reinforcing the intimate feeling that his kiss had awoken. It was an odd reaction, she told herself, for someone on the brink of both poverty and failure. Not to mention that she had just emerged from a very unwise relationship with a man who had managed, quite cleverly, to pull the wool over her eyes. Wool, hell! He had pulled an entire sheep ranch over her totally unsuspecting eyes. That was what falling in love did for you. It made you blind to some very obvious signs. Had she not been in love, she might have been suspicious of some of his actions. Well, all she wanted now was her chance at a career, not electric kisses that made her squirm in her seat.

"I've been performing," she said, trying to sound both professional and distant.

"Have you, now?" he asked with what sounded suspiciously like a patronizing tone.

Dani lifted her chin defensively. "Yes, I have. I'm appearing at a club right now. It's my last night." Now why had she added that? she demanded. That was something she should have told him after a contract had been signed. She didn't want to look like any more of a loser than she already appeared in his eyes.

"Small wonder."

Dani shot a murderous look at the back of Fred's head. Then her look softened as she turned back to Clint. "I'd like you to come and listen to me," she continued, hoping that she didn't sound as if she were begging. She didn't want him to think that she was without pride.

"Where are you singing?" Clint asked.

"The Wild Turkey Saloon," she said. The name

sounded utterly ludicrous now that she said it out loud. She had read that Clint handled people who played the top clubs in Las Vegas, and even the London Palladium. Places like the Wild Turkey never entered into the picture.

"Where?" The word slipped out unintentionally. All he'd meant was that he hadn't heard of the place, but he was sure she would take his question as a slight, and he hadn't meant it as one. He did manage to hold back an amused smile.

Fred held nothing back as a laugh drifted from the front of the limousine.

"The Wild Turkey," Dani repeated, this time pronouncing the words very slowly. "It's a respectable enough place."

Why was she defending it? She hated it. Hated it and the entire string of third-rate places that Jared had booked her into. She had told Jared last night that they were going to have to have a serious talk about where her career was going right after they wound up her gig at the Wild Turkey. That, she told herself, was probably why she had woken up to find everything gone this morning.

"I'm sure it is," Clint answered, and she heard the stifled chuckle in his voice. But she was too desperate to have him come hear her sing to tell him what she thought he could do with his chuckle. She needed this man, and she wasn't going to get him by letting him see that his prospective client had a hot temper. Hot tempers, she reminded herself, were indulgences for the rich and successful, not for the poor and struggling.

"So, will you come?" Dani persisted. Please say yes, her mind pleaded. She felt her fingertips getting cold.

"We sealed the bargain, didn't we?" Clint asked, taking hold of her hand. Icy. Poor kid. Had he done that to her, or was it just poor circulation? "I don't break bargains, especially not those sealed with a kiss." He watched as sweeping dark lashes hooded her brilliant blue eyes. A flicker of what he thought might be embarrassment crossed her features. When her eyes gazed back into his, there was a proud flame in them. He found himself utterly charmed.

"Good. I'll take you no matter how you come—so long as you *do* come," she said firmly.

"I will," he told her.

For some odd reason, she believed him. Maybe she wanted to believe him so much that she wouldn't let herself envision anything else happening. He'd come to the club, he'd be impressed with her regardless of the surroundings, and he'd take her on as a client. From there her career would finally begin to roll.

Fred cleared his throat. As if anyone could forget he was there, Dani thought.

"Can I drop you off somewhere?" Clint asked, looking down into Dani's fresh-scrubbed face. There was great potential there, he decided, beginning to think like an agent again.

Dani glanced down at her watch. It was the only expensive item she owned. Lucky thing she wore it to bed, or else Jared would probably have made off with that, too, she thought. It was five-thirty. She didn't have to go on for another two hours. But if she didn't take advantage of Clint's offer, transportation to the club was going to present a major problem. She didn't want to risk hitchhiking again.

"You can drop me off at the Wild Turkey. It's on East

Keller Street, 121 East Keller Street," she clarified, leaning forward and addressing the back of Fred's head.

Fred's shoulders appeared to tense, as if he were waiting for something, Dani thought. Sure enough, he was.

"It's all right, Fred," Clint told him. Dani watched as the shoulders relaxed ever so slightly while Fred communed once again with the steering wheel.

"What time do you go on?" Clint asked, settling back and once more studying this cross between a wood sprite and Calamity Jane who had entered his life so unceremoniously. "Five-thirty seems a bit early," he observed.

"I find myself temporarily without transportation," Dani answered evasively.

"Car die?" Clint hazarded a guess. She probably drove a beat-up old Chevy that had been cross country nine times under various ownership, he speculated.

"I only wish," Dani muttered, thinking of Jared. She relished the idea of seeing him stranded somewhere.

"I beg your pardon?" The woman was an enigma, no doubt about it. Clint was rather intrigued with solving the puzzle she represented.

Dani shook her blond head. "Nothing. It's a long story," she said with a sigh.

He wanted to hear it and wondered why. Overwork, no doubt. Since Albert had had that heart attack, his own caseload had doubled. He massaged the bridge of his nose, trying to ease the tension he felt. Fred had been warning him about battle fatigue.

"Here, let me," Dani offered after a moment's hesitation. She didn't want to seem overeager, but she *did* want him to see her in a positive light. Besides, if he had a headache, it might make him irritable while he was listening to her. Her whole future could be blown because of a headache.

Before Clint realized what she was offering to do, Dani was applying her long, cool fingers to the outlines of his sinus cavity. With deliberate, rhythmic strokes, she massaged the area above his brow, her touch feathering out to his temple line. She felt him relax beneath her hands, and now it was his turn to sigh. The sigh was one of blissful contentment. It made her reluctant to stop.

What added to her reluctance was the fact that she liked touching his face. In fact, she would have enjoyed letting her fingers explore the rest of his rather fine-boned profile. He wasn't rugged like the men she was used to back home. There, the ones who stayed had the mark of sturdy farmers. This man was the kind that her mother would have called an aristocrat. No, she would have pegged him as a highborn snob, Dani decided. Not that he was delicate looking. What met her approving eyes was quite strong in its own right, but it was strength of character, rather than strength born of pure brawn.

Dani wondered if she could trust him and decided that, for the present, she had no choice. She could only hope that he would keep his word and come to the club later. More than that, she prayed that he would like what he heard. A nervous flutter rose in her stomach, but it didn't get as far as her throat. Nothing ever obstructed that. No matter what happened, Dani always felt that she could go on singing.

The flutters in her stomach took a turn for the worse

when Clint opened his green eyes and looked directly into hers. He had a rather dreamy look.

"You do that very well," he commented.

She could feel his breath on the palm of her hand and wanted to pull it back. But her hand stayed riveted where it was, warmed by his gentle breath. "My mother used to get terrible migraines," she explained. "She always said I had magic hands."

He took one hand in his and pretended to examine it. "Do they perform any other feats of magic?" he asked. The long look he gave her was unnervingly seductive.

Dani grasped at the first thing that came to mind, uncertain of his meaning. "I don't play the guitar," she confessed.

"That's too bad."

From his tone, she didn't think the news really upset him very much.

"This is it," Fred announced, his gravelly voice breaking the sudden stillness in the air.

Fred had stopped the car in front of what looked like a small barn plopped smack in the middle of the city. There was even a hitching post for nonexistent horses.

Dani looked at the front of the saloon and then glanced back at Clint, wondering what he thought of it.

"Quaint," he said for her benefit, feeling that the word was a safe one.

"Dumb" was what Dani had thought the first time she had laid eyes on the place. But the gig paid the bills. Or had promised to.

She became aware of an aura of slight impatience. It was coming from Fred, rather than Clint. Time to leave. "Seven-thirty tonight," she reminded Clint.

He nodded in response.

"You won't forget?" she pressed.

"I won't forget," he promised, his fingers gliding along the length of her hand, sending exciting signals through her body.

As she left the limousine Dani wondered what she was getting herself into.

Watching her go, Clint wondered the same thing.

2

The club was smokier than usual. Noisier, too. Dani's butterflies were breeding at a prodigious rate. She was clutching the microphone so hard that, had it been alive, it would have screamed in protest. She had never been this nervous before. Never.

Damn it, where was he?

She had two songs left before her performance was over. And tonight's crowd wasn't the kind that would encourage an encore. Judging from the looks of some of them, she thought, a wet T-shirt contest would have pleased them far more than an unknown country and western singer.

Of all the places Jared had found, this was by far the worst. The Wild Turkey. What a fitting title for her last public performance. "She died at the Wild Turkey." Dani rolled the caption over in her mind and groaned inwardly. She knew that a lot of performers suffered for their art, but this was going beyond the call of duty. Besides, she had given her word to her parents that if *something* didn't start happening within a year's time, their prodigal daughter would return. Everybody would be happy. Everybody except her.

Of course, she wasn't exactly very happy right now, trying to get the Western-garbed patrons of this dark, smoky establishment to listen to her. She had always felt that she had a voice that would stop people in their tracks and mesmerize them. No such luck here. Well, she had adjusted to that. She would willingly have settled for polite attention. But there was nothing polite about this crowd. They had come to socialize and talk. There might as well have been an inexpensive radio playing in the background.

Her microphone was failing, and the tiny band behind her was playing as if their hearts weren't in it.

What was the use? Who was she fooling? Certainly not them, she thought with a disparaging look at the audience—what she could see of them through the heavy clouds of smoke.

The microphone gave off a piercing squawk, which at least brought a measure of silence, since all eyes turned in her direction. Then the microphone gave up the ghost and died. Conversations began to increase in volume again, and Dani went on singing. She'd finish this song and go. He wasn't coming. He—

He was here! she thought, suddenly seeing him.

Shouldering his way through the crowd, Clint picked out a small, unoccupied beer-stained table and sat down. Still dressed in his expensively tailored blue suit, he looked as out of place as she felt.

Dani's voice swelled, making up for the lack of background music and the dead microphone. The musicians looked at her with renewed interest, took pity and gave it another try. She wasn't sounding half bad for a change, the lead guitarist thought.

Clint was gathering more than his share of looks. He wished he'd had time to change. After he had dropped Dani off, there had been a meeting with a client over an absurdly expensive round of drinks, which he hadn't been able to enjoy because of his client's ill temper. It had taken longer than he expected to iron the matter out. Another man in his place would have gone home and curled his hand around a well-deserved glass of Scotch and soda, putting both his promise and the hopeful country and western singer out of his mind. Clint didn't care for country and western music. Nashville was a long way from San Francisco, and he dealt mainly with actors and supper club performers.

But something about Dani's face had haunted him long after the limousine had left her in front of that ridiculous club in its rundown neighborhood. He had detected a sparkle, a promise of something good. Something big. It might very well be his tired condition, he told himself. And then again, it might not. Fool's gold or the real thing? He had to find out. So he had come to hear her sing.

The waitress who stood over him gave him a slow once-over. A hopeful smile lit her face. "What'll you have, handsome?" she asked in a voice that suffered from too much smoke and one-too-many quickly downed whiskeys.

"Scotch. On the rocks. Neat." Clint placed the order without even looking up at her. He was busy watching

Dani. She had a natural grace despite the situation. The noise level was tremendous. And the band was pretty awful, he thought. But Dani's voice rose above all that, clear and strong. He found himself smiling.

The waitress followed his line of vision. "It's her last night. Maybe they'll get someone with a little life in them next time. Every sweetie-pie-faced kid in fake buckskin thinks she'll be the next Barbara Mandrell."

"Actually, I think the band is rather weak, not the singer," Clint responded thoughtfully.

The waitress shook her head and disappeared into the crowd. It was obvious to her that the stranger had no knowledge of country music. Or else he wasn't really listening to that girl. Her voice was okay, the woman conceded, threading her way through the tide of bodies, but it just didn't ring the bell.

Heartened by the fact that Clint had finally arrived, Dani went on to her last number. A ghost of a melody was heard from her back-up group, who were less than taken with Dani's abilities. They were used to rousing performers who sang toe-tapping music, music that threatened to shake the walls down and get their lease pulled out from under them. All this little blonde did was crying-into-your-beer songs. That was okay once in a while, but not when you wanted to party. Everything in their manner conveyed that message. Dani sensed she was fighting against tremendous odds, but she kept going anyway.

The waitress set down a glass in front of Clint. Still listening to Dani, Clint absently raised it to his lips and took a sip. Watered down. He put the glass back down and realized that the waitress was standing over him expectantly. Digging into his pocket, he found nothing smaller than a fifty, which the waitress took, eyeing both it and him suspiciously. Clint gave her his most reassuring smile. The waitress went for change.

Dani finished. Two or three people clapped absently. Her back-up band retreated without so much as a word to her. The show was over. Was her career over as well? Over before it was born? Dani bit her lip nervously and made her way over to Clint.

Clint rose slightly as Dani took the other seat. For a moment she watched him hesitantly. But nothing was ever won by hesitation, she told herself, so she forged on.

"Well, what did you think?" Thank God for the noise, she thought. That way, he heard the question, but not the accompanying tremor in her voice.

"It was pretty bad," he told her quite honestly.

Dani swallowed. "Well, the microphone died and the audience was rude and the players sounded as if their fingers were getting stuck in the frets, but—" She stopped, sucking in stale air. It was time to face this thing. "*It* was bad or *I* was bad?" She wasn't sure she could stand to hear the answer to her question, and yet she had to know. What this man with the beautiful mouth said would decide her fate for the rest of her life. It was as simple—and as complex—as that.

"I've heard a lot of better singers."

Was that his way of saying she was bad? She tilted her head back, trying to alleviate the tension in the back of her neck. Everything was turning black. "Boy, you sure don't waste words, do you?" she said with a deep edge of bitterness. For the first time since she had started out on this rocky road, she felt like crying. Really crying. Angry, hurt, frustrated, deep, sorry-for-yourself

28

tears. She bit her lip so hard she thought she drew blood. She wasn't about to cry, not in front of this cold fish. Not even if it yielded her a contract. Not even if her life depended on it.

Two fat tears had nowhere to go and coursed down her cheeks anyway.

"Smoke," she lied, turning her head.

Clint nodded, letting her get away with her deception. "Does that to you sometimes," he agreed, feeling terrible. But he had told her the truth. Given the circumstances, of course, Sinatra would have sounded bad, too, he imagined.

Dani rose on wobbly legs. Legs that felt as if they didn't belong to her. "Well, I won't waste any more of your time," she said in a stilted voice. It was all she could manage at the moment. "Thank you for coming."

He reached for her hand, but Dani pulled it back. She didn't want any physical contact. She wanted to go off somewhere and lick her wounds and cry until she died.

"Dani," Clint tried to explain, "I don't manage country and western singers. I—"

"Then why did you come?" she asked accusingly, the hurt finally bursting through its frail restraints. "For a good laugh? Well, mister, I'm going to have the last laugh," she said. She knew she was talking crazy. Her thoughts were scattered. With a major effort, she tried to regroup them and form something that resembled a coherent sentence. "I'm going to be big. So big you'll gnash your teeth because you didn't take me on when you had the chance."

He liked this spitfire better than the weepy woman he had seen a moment ago. "What happened to just trying to earn a living?" he asked, reminding her of what she had said to him earlier.

"That was this afternoon," she informed him with a large measure of bravado. "I've changed my mind!" she announced. "I'm going to be a superstar!" She didn't believe it for one moment, but she hoped she pulled it off well enough that she could at least leave him with doubts.

With that Dani spun on her heel and walked away from him.

She was right, he thought. He'd had no business coming here. He had even less business staying. But he *did* stay, looking into his watered-down Scotch. Had he been too hasty? After all, he *had* been intrigued by her. And though her voice wasn't pure, it did have the beginnings of that special *something* that set performers apart.

He needed another performer like he needed a hole in the head. And yet . . .

Okay, so it hadn't worked, Dani told herself as she pushed unseeingly through the crowd. She had tried a long shot, risked whiplash by leaping into Clint's moving car and had come up empty. There were no guarantees in life. She had become painfully aware of that lately. Maybe it *was* time to pack it all in and go home, despite what she had said to Clint. She was tired of knocking her head against a stone wall, tired of being the only one who believed in herself. She realized all too well now that Jared hadn't believed in her. He had just said the words she wanted to hear, hoping for a free ride. When the big fish in the little pond couldn't manage the transition and become a big fish in the big pond, Jared had bailed out. It was as simple as that. Everyone in American Falls had always told her that she had a fantastic voice. Maybe it was just fantastic for American Falls. Dani sighed.

"Mr. Elliot!" Dani called as the bald-headed owner of the club was about to step into his office.

His head jerked in her direction. He reminded her of a vulture, searching for another victim to prey on. The dark eyes grew a bit darker, or so it seemed in the smoky atmosphere.

"Yeah?"

That was definitely not a friendly voice, Dani thought as she caught up to him. The sooner she was out of here, the happier she'd be.

"This is my last night," Dani reminded him.

A less than heartwarming smile curved the man's fleshy lips. "Yeah, I know." He seemed as relieved about it as she was, except that he wasn't politely trying to hide the fact.

When he didn't respond to the indirect approach, Dani pressed on. "I'm supposed to get paid tonight."

The smile spread. She had a premonition of doom.

"Is that so?" Elliot asked, as if the fact were news to him.

Dani became angry. "Yes, that's so." She glared at him, but he didn't flinch. Could he possibly be thinking of not paying her? she thought in mounting horror.

"Aren't you going to pay me?" Dani finally demanded.

"No," he said, turning his back on her.

For a moment her feet felt as if they were glued to the floor. She heard noises and people all around her, but for all intents and purposes, Dani was standing in a vacuum. This just couldn't be happening to her. Not all at once. What was going on here? Had the world declared war on her?

As if she had been doused with a bucket of cold water, Dani came to just as Elliot began to close the door behind him. She pushed her way in, fortified by smoldering rage rather than normal strength. Adrenaline was a powerful thing.

"We have a contract!" she shouted at him, leaving the door of his crammed, untidy little office open. She was angry, but she wasn't stupid. It was far safer to have an open door with a man like Elliot.

"Have you got it on you?" Elliot shouted back.

"No, I don't have it on me," Dani snapped. "I told you, my manager—"

He didn't let her finish. She had said enough to lay the foundations for his triumph. "No contract, no pay. Simple, kid."

"But we had a deal!" she insisted, picturing her small fist burying itself in his massive stomach. It probably wouldn't have any effect on him, and the thought of coming into such close physical contact with the man made her ill.

"Look, kid, you sang pretty bad," he said, seeing a chance to save himself some money by throwing all the blame on her shoulders. "For all I know, you lost me business. The way I see it, I was doing you a favor lettin' you practice. You," he said, jabbing a pudgy finger into her shoulder, "should've paid me." The thought, newly spawned in his head, struck a spark. "Yeah, you should."

"Trouble, Dani?"

Just as Dani felt herself losing the last of her precious ground, the cavalry came to the rescue, bugles and banners and all. She looked behind her to find the suddenly vastly reassuring frame that belonged to one Clinton A. MacPherson. Her temporary hero. She didn't have to think about it. She just felt it. For one shining instant, she loved him. Gratitude gleamed in her eyes.

"Who's this big guy in the suit?" Elliot demanded, his eyes disappearing into his broad cheeks as he squinted at Clint.

"I'm representing her," Clint announced very quietly. It was the kind of quiet that spoke volumes. It was not wasted on Elliot.

Dani swallowed her gasp of surprise.

Elliot gave the matter one last stab. "Her manager ran off." He cocked his head, glaring at Dani. "What are you trying to pull?" he demanded.

"I'm not her manager, I'm her agent, and the question is, what are *you* trying to pull?" Clint said smoothly, neatly turning the tables. Without looking, he closed the door behind him, locking out the noise. "Dani sang at your rundown establishment and met her end of the bargain. Are you attempting to renege on yours?"

In the face of such eloquent, polished tones and a vocabulary that threatened to lose him at any moment, Elliot decided that it would be far wiser to give up any notions of free entertainment. He puffed up his barrel chest, testing the buttons of his imitation suede vest to their limit. "Are you trying to say I'm welching?" he blustered.

Clint smiled just a little. "I never 'try' to say anything. I state it outright. Pay the lady."

There was no arguing with his tone. Elliot didn't even try. He went directly to his desk and unlocked the deep side drawer where he kept all his receipts.

As the man pulled out a battered strongbox, Dani looked on, watching the minidrama unfold before her. She was at a loss as to what to feel. All sorts of emotions were racing through her. She felt a sense of triumph over having bested Elliot, even though she hadn't actually done it herself. She also felt gratitude toward Clint. And then there was a sense of confusion. Did this mean that he was going to take her on? After what he had just said? But what other explanation could there be for his following her into Elliot's office?

Making Elliot pay her represented two hundred dollars. Having Clint take her on as a client represented a whole lot more. And Dani had just been stung, badly stung, by someone she had trusted. She was still smarting from that. She was leery of trusting anyone else, even if he had practically come riding up on a snow-white charger.

So she stood there, silent, warning herself not to grow too hopeful, while Elliot cursed softly under his breath and counted out two hundred dollars. He had offered to write out a check, but Clint had turned him down. Checks could be stopped. Cash couldn't.

"Nice doing business with you," Clint said over his shoulder as he ushered Dani out of the office. He held onto her elbow and guided her through the swirling crowds of urban cowboys and cowgirls. Not a word was said between them until they were on the street.

He hadn't been able to get her hurt look out of his mind and had followed her when she had disappeared into Elliot's office. When he heard how the man was trying to cheat her, Clint had stepped in. Feisty though she seemed, she needed someone to take care of her. Somehow, he had found himself volunteering.

Dani looked up at Clint as he let go of her elbow. A sense of emptiness pervaded her as he withdrew his hand. "Thank you," she finally said after a few false starts.

"Any time," Clint said gallantly. "Give you a lift?" he offered.

Dani nodded and let him lead the way to the limousine. "Did you mean that?"

"Mean what?"

"About any time?" she clarified.

His common sense suffered a major defeat as he answered, "Sure."

"Does that mean," she pressed on, "that you've changed your mind about taking me on?"

He didn't answer her question, because something else had drawn attention away from her. Fred and his car had attracted a ring of people who were circling the long black limousine. It looked sorely out of place on a street that was lined with pick-up trucks and economy cars.

"Time to go, Fred," Clint announced, his tall frame slicing neatly through the crowd.

"About time you got here," Fred muttered, getting back into the dark vehicle.

Dani felt a little like a princess stepping into her coach as Clint ushered her inside, then closed the door behind her.

"You make a habit out of rescuing people?" Dani couldn't resist asking as Clint slid in next to her.

Clint chuckled. "Sure. I belong to the honorary Lone Ranger Club. Want to see my silver bullet?" he offered, his eyes twinkling.

It was her turn to laugh. "No, I'll take your word for

it." The mood turned serious with her next statement. "You never did answer my question about representing me."

"No, I didn't," he agreed, making no further comment.

"Well, will you?" she cried, not being able to stand this any longer.

"I'm not sure yet," he said honestly, wrestling with the issue. He saw a great deal of potential in her, but did he really have the time to develop it? "Let me think about it, okay?"

What choice did she have? Dani shrugged. "Okay." At least the situation was beginning to sound more positive than it had back in the Wild Turkey.

Clint felt her shoulders sag against his, and for the first time in a long time, he felt a pang of guilt. She thought he was brushing her off, he realized. Suddenly he longed to make her smile, but he cautioned himself against being too hasty.

Beneath her fire and spunk, Dani did indeed need him, just as she had said when she had come sailing into his limousine. Funny thing about the word "need," he thought. It not only generated a sense of responsibility, but a sense of intimacy. It cut through the formalities and barriers that strangers set up against one another.

Strangest of all, Clint felt that he liked being needed by this aspiring sagebrush singer.

He realized that he had been silent for too long a time, and that both Fred, who had come to a halt several blocks away from the club, and Dani, were looking at him. He needed to give Fred a destination. "Where are you staying?" he asked Dani.

"The Happy Traveler," Dani answered, none too

thrilled about making the fact public. When she had first seen the rows of tiny cabins, she had decided that the motel's name had evolved out of the fact that the traveler in question was happy to travel on, leaving the establishment in his wake. It was by far the worst in the string of dismal places where she had been forced to take refuge.

"Never heard of it," Clint admitted.

She looked at him with his expensive suit, his hundred-dollar haircut and his handmade shirt. He most definitely had the aura of both money and success about him. Why would he have heard of the Happy Traveler? "It's on Magnolia and Richmond," she told him.

"Fred . . ." Clint began without bothering to finish his sentence.

"Another pass into the unknown," Fred muttered rather audibly as he turned the car's long, black frame in the general direction of the streets Dani had mentioned.

"Been at this long?" Clint asked, finding that he wanted to know more about Dani, even though he felt it was an unwise move. The more he knew, the harder it was going to be to finally say no to her. And, after all, besides his full list of clients, there was the fact that he didn't handle her type of music. Truthfully, neither did she. She wasn't suited for the type of material she was doing. Some performers were born to be in their fields. They were natural singers, dancers, actors and so on. But some gave the audience an uncomfortable feeling, as if they were trying to pull on a dress that was too tight, or wear shoes that were too large. Something just didn't fit right. That was how he had felt watching Dani perform. She was selling her soul without any takers. And yet . . . Yet there was something there. Something he didn't have the time to analyze.

"Singing?" Dani asked, breaking into his thoughts to answer the question he had asked her. "Forever," she answered. "My mother said I sang before I talked."

Clint nodded politely. Mothers of would-be performers were wont to say things like that. It sounded good—or so they thought.

"No, I meant publicly. For money," he added.

"Oh." Dani sighed, sinking deeper into the leather seat. "Eleven months." Eleven months and nothing to show except the embarrassment of being left without anything. Dani's feeling of bitterness grew.

"Have they all been like . . . ?"

"Like the Wild Turkey? Mostly," she admitted. "Jared, my manager, was as new at this as I was."

Clint saw the way her mouth hardened as she pronounced the other man's name. Had there been something between them? Something that had hurt her? He felt compelled to press on. "Then you have a manager," he concluded.

"Had," she corrected. The word was so brittle that it practically splintered as she spoke it.

"Had?"

Dani looked at Clint, not wanting to admit to a total stranger that she had been abandoned. Would he want to take on a loser? Still, she had to let someone know sooner or later. She felt as if she were going to explode if the words stayed inside. "He ran out on me this morning. Took the money he was 'holding' for me. Took the van. Took everything."

Here she was, practically abandoned on his doorstep with a note pinned to her blanket saying, "Take care of me," Clint thought. The word "no" was getting harder and harder to hang onto. Still, it might all be a ruse. Cleverer ones had been used on him.

He looked down into her face. Somehow, he told himself, someone with eyes that blue and clear couldn't lie.

"In this business," he told her, momentarily taking refuge behind well-worn words, "you have to be extremely careful. It seems to attract the most unscrupulous sort of people. . . ."

"So I've noticed," Dani replied, her usually lively voice so flat, so devoid of emotion, that it was startling.

The limousine's tires sank into coarse gravel as Fred pulled into the driveway of the Happy Traveler Motel.

"This is it?" Clint asked, pressing a button on the armrest. The darkly tinted window rolled down. Poking his head out and taking a clearer look at the sight before him didn't change his first impression. The place looked better from behind a tinted window.

"This is Magnolia and Richmond," Fred told his employer without turning around. Having been with both Senior and Junior for thirty years, Fred almost sensed what was coming next. He knew what Clint was going to say before Clint did.

The cabins were little better than shanties. "I wouldn't board my dog in a kennel that looked like this," Clint said. Too late he realized how his words must have sounded to Dani.

She sat up a little straighter. "Your dog would undoubtedly have more to spend than I do. Besides," she added with false cheerfulness, "it's not so bad. The larger bugs are freshly laundered once a week." She put her hand on the door and pulled the handle. The door didn't budge. So much for a dramatic exit, she thought as she tugged futilely once again. "Okay," she said, turning back to Clint, "how do I get out of this thing?"

"You don't," he declared, making a decision. "You're coming home with me."

Dani stared at him, wide-eyed.

Fred sighed in resignation. He'd known it all along.

3

Somehow Dani found her tongue. "I beg your pardon?" She had heard of fast operators, but this guy was in a class by himself.

"I said you're coming home with me," Clint repeated, slightly surprised to hear the words himself. "I wouldn't let my worst enemy stay in a place like this. And since you're not my worst enemy," he said, shifting his shimmering green gaze in her direction, "you're coming with me."

Dani wasn't sure just how to react to this offer. Logic told her that the man was probably out for an easy evening. Instinct told her something else.

"Just because I'm from Idaho," she began cautiously, not wanting to offend him, yet wanting to make everything perfectly clear from the start, "doesn't mean that I'm a hick."

Her remark threw him for a moment. "What does that have to do with living in a pigsty?"

"Nothing, but . . ."

The light dawned. "Oh." The light was followed by a grin. One of the most charming Dani had ever seen. One that, she sensed, would someday lead to her undoing if she weren't careful. "Not to worry Miss Christopher," Clint continued. "You'll be properly chaperoned. Fred lives with me."

In response, Fred half turned in her direction.

The fact that Fred lived with Clint did not alleviate Dani's sense of uneasiness in the slightest. What did he care what his esteemed boss did with a singer who appeared to be down on her luck?

"It's not that I'm not grateful—" Dani began. She never got any further.

"Good," Clint interrupted, getting out of the car. "Then let's get you out of here before you catch something." He took hold of her hand, and Dani found herself following mutely.

She took the lead and brought him to a small building that looked like a crumbling sugar cube. It was badly in need of both paint and repairs. Stale, musty air greeted them when she opened the door. As if in a dream, Dani walked over to the closet. She pulled the graffiti-covered door open, took out her suitcase and began filling it with her clothes. It took her all of five minutes.

"That's all there is?" Clint asked, looking down at the lone, shabby suitcase.

"I travel light," she replied, wondering if she was making a mistake. But then, she had already made a mistake, trusting Jared. Wasn't it time for something good to come her way?

"Obviously," he laughed. "Isn't there anything else,

though?" He knew women who wouldn't travel to a restaurant without more paraphernalia than that.

Dani shook her head. "This is it. All my worldly goods," she added wryly.

Clint smiled in response to her words. The more he knew about her, the more he liked her.

"C'mon, let's go," he said, reaching for the suitcase.

But Dani pulled it back. "That's okay. I'll carry my own load, thanks." It was her small stab at independence. Dumb, she knew, but necessary. At least for her.

Clint let it pass. "Where's the proprietor of this glowing establishment?" he asked as he held the door open for her.

"Up front."

He followed her to the first shack. The sound of a ballgame in progress, complete with armchair coaching, could be heard long before they entered the squat building. The screen door banged behind them, hanging drunkenly from its one secure hinge.

"Yeah?" the matted-looking man growled, tossing the word in their general direction, his eyes riveted to the blurred colors on the fifteen-inch screen.

"We'd like to take care of the lady's bill if you don't mind," Clint said, a clear note of impatience in his voice. He wasn't used to addressing the back of someone's uncombed head.

"Mind?" A beery laugh gurgled out of the recesses of the man's throat. "Mister, that's the name of the game." Keeping one eye on the set at all times, the burly man flipped open the worn, stained register. "Hey, you're that little girl in Bungalow 19," he said in sudden recognition. He had seen Jared pulling out in the middle of the night and had surmised the rest, tossing in his own grisly details. He looked Clint up and down. "See you've found yourself another one fast enough," he said to Dani.

If floors could have been willed to open and swallow people up on command, Dani would have vanished from the spot, glowing pink cheeks and all. But the floor and Dani stayed just where they were. But before she could tell the hulking man in the T-shirt what she thought of him, his tattoo, his establishment and life in San Francisco in general, Clint spoke up.

"I'm the lady's agent," he clarified, and his words put the man in his place neatly. "Now, if you don't mind, she's in rather a hurry. I have an important audition scheduled for her. I take it the bill hasn't been paid."

Dani's head jerked in Clint's direction at the mention of an audition. But then she realized that he was just saying that for effect, and she felt grateful to him. She looked back at the burly man behind the desk, allowing just the tiniest bit of smugness to come through.

There was no arguing with the authority in Clint's voice. The leering man was reduced to the role of a scraping peon as he hastily wrote up Dani's bill and handed the paper to her. "That guy only paid for his room."

Clint intercepted the bill. "The price of shanties is high these days," he commented, pulling out his wallet. He tossed the man a hundred dollar bill. The man stared at it as if it were a live grenade. People who filled their wallets with hundred-dollar bills did not frequent his motel. "It's genuine," Clint assured him, then turned and escorted Dani out.

"I can take care of my own bills," Dani told Clint as soon as they were outside.

He didn't even acknowledge her statement. "I didn't like what he was implying about you."

44

He sounded like a knight in shining armor, Dani thought. But knights didn't exist anymore. She was going to have to be very careful around him. It would be too easy to fall under his spell, and she was through with spells, she told herself firmly. Still, she felt a grateful tenderness toward him glowing inside her.

They arrived at the car to find Fred leaning against it, his arms crossed over his barrel chest. "So, you're going through with this," was the only comment he made before he let them into the limousine, then got in himself. He was shaking his head as he did so.

"Home, Fred." Clint instructed.

"You don't really have an audition set up for me—do you?" Dani asked, groping for something to talk about. She knew he couldn't possibly have one. After all, he wasn't even sure if he was taking her on yet.

"Yes."

The answer surprised her. How? When? "With whom?"

"Me."

Dani's back stiffened and her eyes narrowed. "What kind of an audition?" she asked warily.

"I thought all they raised in Idaho were potatoes, not suspicious women," he said wryly. His manner sobered a bit. "I want you to sing for me," he told her honestly, a thought forming in his head.

"For my supper?" she asked, an old nursery rhyme suddenly coming to mind.

"For your future," he corrected. "I'll feed you tonight, no matter what. Provided that Fred remembered to do the shopping today." He looked into the rearview mirror, catching Fred's eye. Fred nodded grudgingly. "Good," Clint said. "We eat."

This was all getting too confusing for Dani. "You heard me sing in the club," she pointed out.

"Yes," Clint said with a sigh. "I did. But I'm beginning to get a different image now, fortunately."

"What sort of an image?" She wanted to know.

"I'm not quite sure yet," he answered honestly. He saw the suspicious look begin to rise in her eyes again. "Bear with me, okay?" He reached out and patted her hand.

Put that way, Dani felt as if she could have borne with anything—for the time being. There was something inherently likable about Clint, despite all Dani's newly born caution. This morning she had been given a harsh lesson about the rude realities of the world around her. What was transpiring here felt as if it belonged in a fairy tale. Was her luck changing at last? Or was this going to be the biggest disaster of all?

She tried not to think, and turned to face the window. Lights beckoned from every direction as they wound their way up Telegraph Hill. Despite the hour, or perhaps because of it, the area was bursting with activity. Attractive restaurants all up and down the Hill were being patronized by wealthy people in search of a culinary treat. Or perhaps just in search of a way to pass their evening.

Must be nice, Dani thought in silent envy. Well, maybe someday . . .

Eventually Fred brought the car to a halt before a pier-front condominium. The building was a beautiful combination of gray-blue wood and stucco.

"Home?" Dani guessed, craning her neck as she looked up at the two-story building.

"Home," Clint confirmed, getting out.

She took his hand without seeing it, still looking at the

building. "Boy, some people sure know how to live," she muttered under her breath.

He laughed, taking pleasure in her innocent, awed reaction. "If that's a compliment, thank you," he answered, his voice low. She wasn't sure if it was his tone or the cool ocean breeze that made her shiver.

Fred went to put the limo in the garage, while Clint took Dani's arm and led her up the steps to the front door. Dani looked at him hesitantly, wondering if she should turn tail and run. Was she making a mistake?

Clint caught the worried look that crossed her brow. He took her hand. "It's warmer inside."

"I don't doubt it," she answered. It brought a smile to his lips. "My suitcase," she said, suddenly remembering, and turned toward the garage. She was half ready to run and retrieve it. Anything to buy herself some time.

"Fred will bring it in," Clint assured her, placing the palm of his hand between her shoulder blades to guide her into the house.

It was a warm house, as warm and tasteful as the man who owned it. Cream tile flecked with gold lay in the foyer, leading the eyes toward an open, winding stairway. She had never known anyone with a winding stairway. She was beginning to think that she had never known anyone quite like Clint.

"Where's your dog?" she asked, looking around. She couldn't picture one scampering around on the white tile.

"I don't have one."

She turned to look at him in surprise. "But you said—"

"Poetic license," he explained with a smile.

"Oh."

47

"Family room's this way," Clint went on briskly, pointing toward his right. "Beyond that's the kitchen and the dining room. On the other side—" he nodded toward his left "—are the living room, the video room and one of the guest rooms. There are three more bedrooms upstairs."

"Must keep you busy." The remark escaped before she realized what she was saying. With a hooded side glance, she looked at Clint's face to see his reaction.

He appeared to be tickled. "I only use my own," he said significantly.

Fred came in through the side entrance, shutting the door behind him and mumbling incoherently under his breath as he walked up to Dani and placed the suitcase at her feet.

"Put it in the room next to mine, Fred," Clint instructed. "And then check on dinner."

"Nothing to check. It's not made yet," Fred muttered, picking up the worn valise again. The thing looked to him as if it had been used in a commercial comparing the way different brands of luggage weathered travel. This was brand X.

"There goes the soul of cooperation." Clint laughed affectionately. He turned his attention back to Dani. She was still dressed in the same absurd outfit he had first seen her in. "I'm sorry. I'm forgetting my manners. Would you like to go upstairs and change?" he suggested.

Dani immediately felt both self-conscious and defensive. "Why?" she asked, looking down at herself and seeing nothing wrong. "I thought if I was going to sing for you, I might as well dress for it."

Clint shook his head. "Not that way. You're not meant for country and western," he told her firmly. As

48

he said the words aloud, he realized just how right he was. The two were totally mismatched.

Dani was mystified. All her life she had turned to radio stations where the announcers had a twang in their voices, listening to singers bemoan lost lovers, unfaithful mates and a shortage of beer. She couldn't picture herself singing anything else. "What would you know about it?" she challenged, even though logic instructed her to hold her tongue. "You said you don't handle country and western singers."

"I *don't* handle them," he agreed, although there was something about her that certainly made him entertain very pleasant ideas about handling her—in every sense of the word.

"Then what are you doing with me?" she finally asked in bewilderment. There were some things that just had to get defined here.

"I don't know," he muttered under his breath.

"What?" She hadn't heard him.

"Forget it," he advised. Carelessly, he slipped an arm around her fringed shoulders. "Let's just say that after a very long time in the business, I do have a kind of sixth sense about what goes and what doesn't in the world of entertainment. If you stick to your routine, you'll be doomed to playing honky-tonks for the rest of your life, competing with smoke, noise and, ultimately, the cackle of chickens." He led her into the study.

Dani didn't even realize she was walking. Her adrenalin level was up. Who was he to downgrade her to that degree? Okay, so he was a top talent agent. But what did he know of dreams? Or wanting something so bad that your soul hurt when you thought about not having it? From the way he looked, she'd wager that everything had always come easily to him.

"Okay," she said slowly, measuring out her words, "what *do* you think I'm good for?"

For holding on a bright, moonlit night. The thought flashed across his mind, and he tucked it away with a smile. That would really send her packing, and right now he didn't want her to go. He wasn't sure what he was going to do with her, but he had liked the quality of her voice. Besides, his instincts told him that, with the right direction, she could be someone. She had a certain inner quality that made him believe she was marketable. Very marketable. Her wide doe-eyes bored into his soul.

"I don't know—yet," he said honestly, putting his hands on her shoulders and sitting her down. He had given up the idea of letting her go and change. "But I'm going to find out."

"What does that mean?" Nervousness, fear and anticipation licked at her stomach from all sides. She wasn't sure exactly what she was expecting as she watched him walk to the far side of the room.

The entire wall was devoted to an elaborate stereo system. Clint thumbed through his vast record collection. "That means I'm going to listen to you sing without hearing some guy order a boilermaker in the background." He found what he was looking for. In his youth, they had called this kind of thing make-out music. It was airy, dreamy, guaranteed to soften and yet stir the soul. He glanced at Dani, not seeing the glittering outfit that hung on her body. This was what she was meant for, unless he missed his guess. And he rarely missed his guess.

"Do you know the words to this one?" he asked, pointing to an instrumental selection on the album.

Dani bent closer, reading the title. "Sure," she told Clint, looking back up. It was an old standard. "But why? . . ."

He went back to the stereo, set the album on the turntable and carefully placed the needle by the right selection. "Never ask me why, Dani. There isn't always an answer. Just a feeling." He chose a comfortable chair and leaned back. He looked relaxed, but in reality every one of his nerve endings was alert, waiting. "Sing."

Dani felt like a puppet on a string. Worse than that, she wasn't used to this kind of a melody. But she took off her jacket and did her best, pretending that this was an audition. The music enveloped her, pulling at something within her. Soon she found herself flowing with the words she was singing.

"Love me, my love, and we'll sail away,
On moonbeams,
and dewdrops,
and ocean spray.

Come with me and we'll fly
On a butterfly's wing.
Ours will be a world of youth,
Of eternal spring.

Love me, my love, and there's nothing
I cannot do.
Love me, my love,
only half as much as I love you.

Love me, my love.
Quickly, before our world fades away.

Love me, my love.
  Not tomorrow,
  Today.
  Today!"

Dani stopped, the haunting refrain over, but still echoing in the otherwise silent room and enchanting them both. For a moment their eyes met and held as bittersweet emotion tugged at them. Dani felt, for that solitary moment, as if she had sung the song to him. As if she needed to sing the song to him. The next moment, reality seeped in and she was the first to break the spell. She had gotten carried away with the song, that was all. That, and with the discovery that she liked a new type of music.

"Well, what did you think?" she asked, her nerves taut. An unfamiliar tune played softly in the background. She liked the melody. It was warm and sensuous. Like Clint.

Clint rose slowly to his feet, coming to join her. "Don't look so tense," he told her, taking her hand. He gently sat her down on the sofa next to him. "You need work," he said truthfully.

She had hoped he was going to say she was terrific. For some reason, his opinion had suddenly come to mean a lot. She told herself it was because he was an important agent. Deliberately, she shut the door on the fact that there was something more, something small and struggling, but something more nonetheless.

"That doesn't sound very promising," she said with a growing note of despair.

"On the contrary," he said. "That's very promising. What wasn't promising was the routine you were performing at the Crazy Chicken—"

"—Wild Turkey," she corrected, holding back a smile.

"Whatever." Clint shrugged. "You're not cut out to sing crying-into-your-beer songs," he told her flatly. "That would be a waste and a shame. Your voice is too sultry. And," he went on, his finger tracing a line from her neckerchief down along the V formed by her rows of fringes, "I suspect that beneath all those spangles and fringes there's a sultry body to go along with the voice."

Dani felt her heart hammering hard just beneath the point where his finger stayed poised. "That's for me to know," she retorted a bit too quickly. And for you to find out, an inner voice, one she tried to ignore, added.

Clint smiled. "That's not what I meant," he told her. "I'm talking about costumes, not the lack of them."

She flushed, embarrassed at having shown him where her thoughts had immediately fled. What was the matter with her? She had just gotten over a very bad experience; she'd had her affections used against her and thrown in her face. What was she doing, leaving herself open to the same thing again? Was she crazy? This was going to be a professional relationship. Strictly professional.

Dani saw a shimmer rising in Clint's green eyes. The hell it was, she thought helplessly.

In the background, the record came to a halt as the needle lifted, then returned to the first song. Clint had failed to place the restraining arm down. They might very well be surrounded by dreamy music for the rest of the evening.

Somehow, there were worse fates to suffer, Dani thought as she watched Clint's irresistible face draw near. The scent of his after-shave wafted toward her, rendering her even more vulnerable than she already was.

One very strong, yet gentle hand cupped her cheek and the underside of her chin. Sparks ignited all through her body. He tilted her head ever so slightly, his long, dark lashes veiling his intense green eyes. And then he kissed her. Again.

Whatever he had stirred within her the first time was there waiting the second time around. There was no need to build up to it. It was not only there, it had heightened. The pressure of his mouth on hers was the most exciting sensation she had ever experienced. And she wanted it to go on forever.

It drained her of all thought, made her forget all her vows to separate work and play, made her forget that she had decided never to play again. All she knew, all she felt, was that she loved what was happening. This wasn't a kiss. This was rapture in its purest form.

Dani could feel the heat of his body as he drew her closer to him, his free arm slipping around her shoulders. The hand that had framed her face drifted down to her neck, the fingers spreading lightly along her throat, making the pulse he found dance to the tune he played. An ache spread from the center of her body, making her sway with desire.

Clint's fingers rested on the top of her dress, then slid a little lower, held in check by the shiny material. He did not press further, but Dani felt as if he could burn the cloth away with the heat of his hand. She wanted him to touch her, to hold her, to make love to her. She was lost in his kiss, craving fulfillment.

A very unceremonious cough cracked the euphoric atmosphere of love songs and deepening emotions.

"You two still want to eat?" Fred asked. "Or do you want to put dinner on hold?"

Dani sprang back from Clint. Or tried to. One of the longer glistening fringes on her dress had gotten caught on his tie tack, and she didn't get far. Dani avoided both men's eyes as she yanked her fringe free. A piece of fabric remained behind on the tack. A trophy, she thought cynically.

Get a rein on yourself, girl. You want to make the *Guinness Book of World Records* for being a fool twice in twenty-four hours?

"You have a wonderful way with words, Fred," Clint commented as he rose, totally unruffled. "Dinner will be fine. Dani?" he asked, looking down at her. He offered her his hand.

God, he sounded as if nothing had happened. Hadn't he felt anything? Hadn't he experienced the fire that had claimed her? No, apparently not, she decided, ignoring his hand and getting up by herself.

She walked stiffly in front of him as Fred led the way to the dining room. Clint was a man who dealt in beautiful women the way salespeople dealt in merchandise. With gorgeous women on all sides of him, why would he be expected to feel something for an Idaho sweet potato? she thought dryly.

Cool down, she ordered herself.

Easier said than done, her mind responded.

4

The dining room took her breath away. The dining rooms Dani had known were either simple off-shoots of the living room, or closely nestled next to the kitchen, filled with warmth, noise and clutter. This large, dark wood-paneled room seemed to indicate that its inhabitants should speak in whispers. A chandelier hung overhead, casting a somber light.

The table was long and massive. The towering hutch was filled with china. All this combined to make Dani feel very small and inconsequential, not warm and secure the way the rest of the house did. She noted with relief that her place setting was next to Clint's, instead of at the other end of the table. Clint held out her chair, and she gave him a small smile as she slid in, suddenly feeling very awkward. Her spangles and fringes were definitely out of place here, amid all this hushed wealth.

Clint sensed her discomfort and was intrigued by it. Most of the people he knew were either born to something like this, or very eager to attain it. At the very least, they would have made a show of fitting in. Dani was quietly hovering on the outside, peering in like a child through a candy store window. He wanted to put her at ease.

"Tell me about yourself," Clint urged quietly as Fred returned with the salad.

"Nothing much to tell," she answered automatically. She was certain that, in comparison to his, her life was deadly dull. She would rather leave him wondering about it than confirm any suspicions he might have.

Dani reached for a fork and found an array of silver at her disposal. Several forks of varying sizes lay under her hand. Feeling inadequate again, she sighed softly. Which one was she supposed to use?

When she glanced up, she saw Clint watching her. She tried to tell whether he was just amused, or feeling sorry for her because she didn't know which fork went with which course. He smiled, picked up a fork and began to eat. Dani retrieved the corresponding one on her side. One hurdle passed, she thought.

"If I'm to be your agent, I'd like to know what I'm getting myself into," Clint said.

Her fork stopped in midair. "Then you are going to represent me?" she asked, her voice rising an octave. Her enthusiasm netted a "Knew it all along," from Fred, who had just entered, carrying the main course.

Dani was so happy that she even forgave Fred his dour expression. She stifled an impulse to throw her arms around Clint. She had done that once—no, twice. She couldn't keep doing it and expect their relationship to remain strictly professional. She had only been in his company for a total of a few hours, and already she felt extremely attracted to him.

No, that was just her raw vulnerability coming to the fore, she told herself, exploring her feelings no further. She was too happy, too relieved. She felt like singing, like hugging the whole world. It was only natural that she should feel some sort of attraction, even affection, for the man who was responsible for her happiness.

He saw the joy she felt glowing in her eyes, her face, her very being. He marveled at how very little it took to make her happy. He hadn't promised to make her a star, only to help direct her career. Things might not even turn out, he thought philosophically. But she was looking at him as if he were Santa Claus and had just handed her his entire sack of toys. Clint felt something he hadn't experienced in a long, long time. He felt a wave of tenderness wash over him.

Only Fred seemed to maintain a dark air. He set the loaded down platter he'd been carrying between Clint and Dani, then gave Clint a warning look, but for once he said nothing.

"Why doesn't he like me?" Dani asked as soon as Fred had left the room. Fred's obvious disapproval hadn't dampened her elation, but it did confuse her a little. She didn't think she had done anything to merit it.

"Fred thinks I have too many clients as it is," Clint said, pushing the remainder of his salad aside. He nodded at the piping hot roast, casting a questioning glance in her direction.

"Please," Dani said in response to his silent inquiry. He began to cut several slices for her. She watched, unseeing, as she chewed on her lip. Her curiosity got the better of her tact. "Isn't he a little out of line, mumbling like that?" she asked. "I mean, I know I'm the last person in the world to talk about being out of line, leaping into your car like that, but . . ."

He had a feeling that, if he let her, she'd ramble on for several minutes, searching for the proper way to make her point without placing the proverbial foot in her mouth. He came to her rescue. "Fred and I have a rather strange relationship."

"Oh."

It was a very pregnant "oh," and when he looked at her, her eyes were riveted to her plate. He couldn't help chuckling, wondering what someone as innocent as she was considered a "strange relationship." He thought he knew and was quick to set her mind at rest.

"He thinks he's my mother."

Dani's eyes shot up to his face. She swallowed the piece of meat she was chewing. "What?" The meat suddenly halted midway down her throat, and she began to cough.

Clint was on his feet immediately, giving her a resounding thump on her back and offering her the goblet next to her plate. She hastily took a large swallow before she realized that the liquid in the glass was not water but white wine. She stared up at him with surprised, watery eyes. "This isn't water!" she cried.

"No, it's wine," he replied. "Are you all right?"

She cleared her throat and nodded. "Other than being embarrassed," she admitted in a high voice, "yes."

He made no comment, and she was grateful for that. As if nothing had happened, he went on talking. "I think Fred's was the first face I saw staring down at me in my bassinet."

"That's too bad," she murmured, thinking that

Fred's expression was enough to frighten any baby. And then she grinned.

"What is it?" Clint asked, wanting to share the joke.

"I was just picturing you in back of the limousine at about five, having Fred chauffeur you around."

He laughed. "He was chauffeuring my father around then. What he did with me was take care of me," he told her. Dani was leaning her head on her upturned palm, totally ignoring her food. She enjoyed listening to him talk about himself.

Clint went on talking, revealing more than he usually did to any client. But then, theirs was an unusual client/agent relationship, he thought dryly. He rarely entertained his clients in his home. His home was his sanctuary. And somehow the word "sanctuary" seemed fitting just now. Despite the fierce front she presented, Dani needed a sanctuary, he thought.

"There were governesses, of course," he said, "but it was Fred who actually took care of me."

"But what about your mother?" Dani blurted out before good sense told her to hold her tongue. "I'm sorry," she said hastily. "I have no right to . . ."

He waved her words away graciously. "My mother died in a car accident when I was five." The sorrow that came into Dani's eyes was genuine, and Clint was touched by it. It made him remember his own pain. He had successfully buried it long ago, or so he had thought. "My father had a promising business to run. He hired a string of governesses. All kindly ladies, each with her own set of rules. None of them lasted very long around Fred, though. He thought he could do a better job himself." Clint grinned. "Eventually my father gave up trying to get someone and handed my care and feeding over to Fred. Only trouble is," he said, picking up his own wineglass, "Fred doesn't like relinquishing his duties. More wine?" he asked.

Dani shook her head so hard that her hair bounced against her cheeks, framing her face with caressing blond tendrils. Clint felt an urge to brush them aside, to feel the softness of her cheek beneath his fingers.

"I didn't even want the wine I had," she answered.

She felt giddy and was beginning to have difficulty separating fantasy from the real world. Was she actually being wined and dined by a knight in shining armor, or rather, an agent in an expensive blue suit? Could all this really be happening to her at long last? Someone had once told her never to drink alcohol on an empty stomach, and except for the few leaves of lettuce and the one misdirected piece of roast beef, she had had nothing to eat all day. She had been too depressed to eat. But all that seemed light-years away right now. Everything seemed light-years away except for the man who sat beside her. Dani wondered how much of the elation she felt was due to the wine and how much was because of him.

"I seem to be the one going down memory lane," Clint said, and she thought she detected a touch of self-consciousness in his voice. "My original question, before the subject of Fred came up, was about you. Everyone has something to tell about themselves," he prompted. "I want to know about you. Albert will undoubtedly make you write up a bio before the week is out."

"Albert?" she asked.

"Albert Reynolds. My partner. He's semiretired now, but his rules aren't." Suddenly he remembered something. "Oh, God, I forgot." He glanced at his watch.

"Forgot what?" she asked, watching him quickly rise.

"I'm supposed to be meeting with one of his clients. He couldn't make it." He frowned. It wasn't like him to forget something like that. But Dani and her doelike eyes had made him forget almost everything. He was going to have to watch himself in the future. Business and pleasure were a fatal mixture in this line of work. He had to remain distant.

"Fred!" he called out, and Fred materialized instantly.

"Dessert?" he asked.

"No, I forgot about Constance Benoit," Clint said.

"Most people would like to," was Fred's response.

"*The* Constance Benoit?" Dani asked in a hushed whisper. "The one with the three Academy Awards?"

Clint flashed her a smile. "The one with the temper that explodes when she thinks she's being ignored." He turned toward Fred. "Stay here with Dani, I'll take the Mercedes."

Fred, Dani could see, didn't look exactly thrilled with his assignment.

"Oh, I'll be all right," she began quickly. The look on Fred's face stopped her from continuing. His skin was tanned and leathery, with creases etched into his cheeks. He frowned a lot, she surmised. Just like he was now. Probably the less she said the better. She turned her attention toward the roast beef.

"Fred'll show you to your room when you're finished," Clint told her, hurrying out, Fred at his heels. "Sorry about this."

She gave him a fleeting smile, and then he was gone. Feeling suddenly lonely, she sat listening to the sounds of Clint moving away.

The gaping hole she had so recently discovered in her stomach was suddenly, unaccountably, filled by less than enough food to sustain a canary. She pushed her plate away.

"What's the matter? Don't you like it?"

Dani jumped, so startled that her chair wobbled dangerously beneath her.

"I—I didn't hear you come back," she stammered, looking at Fred, who stood in the doorway.

"Obviously." He came into the room and looked at the plate expectantly. "So what's wrong with the meal?" he asked doggedly. It was a good word to use to describe him. He made her think of a bulldog. An old bulldog whose territory had just been invaded.

She tried to smile at him. "There's nothing wrong with it. It's delicious. I'm just . . . not hungry." Her voice faded with the words.

Fred was swift to clear the plate away. "Do you want dessert?" he practically snapped.

"No," she said quietly, then decided that she had cowered enough. "What are you so angry about?" she asked.

"I'm not angry," he said, walking out.

Dani followed him into the wide, bright kitchen. Decorative pots hung overhead, their gleaming copper surfaces reflecting the light into her eyes. The room was so clean that it almost hurt to look at it, but it was too antiseptic for her taste.

"You are *too* angry," she insisted when he turned demanding dark eyes on her. "What's the matter?" she asked nervously, refusing to back down.

"I'm not used to having Mr. MacPherson's guests follow me into the kitchen," he said crisply. "And I'm *not* angry," he repeated. "This is my normal manner."

The smart thing to do was retreat and wait quietly in the dining room until Fred deigned to take her up to her room. Dani wasn't the bravest soul in the world, but she couldn't picture herself hiding in corners, keeping out of Fred's way during her stay, so she slid onto a white stool, propped her elbows on the counter and leaned her head on her hands. Fred gave her a disapproving look.

"You should try smiling for a change. That way you won't frighten people so much," she told him.

"I *like* frightening people," he told her, lifting the almost untouched roast beef and placing it on another platter. "That way," he went on, covering the platter, "they don't stand around, pestering me."

"Okay," she said, annoyed. "You don't have to hit me over the head with a two-by-four." She wasn't intimidated, she was angry, and it showed on her face. With a quick movement, she jumped off the stool. Unfortunately, her exit wasn't as smooth as she would have liked it to be. The stool tipped over, caught on several of her fringes. She crouched down, trying to disengage herself from the overturned stool.

To her surprise, Fred came around the bar and pushed her fingers out of the way. "I'll do it," he announced irritably. "That dress of yours is lethal," he groused. "First you get yourself stuck to the boss, then you turn the stool into a pull toy."

"Doesn't it make you feel funny?" she asked out of the blue.

He looked at her, bewildered. For a moment the perpetual scowl was gone. "What, yanking on your dress?"

"No, calling Clint 'boss.' He told me that you practically raised him."

"He said that?"

64

He sounded so surprised that Dani asked the natural question that came into her mind. "Yes. Isn't it true?"

"Oh—" another yank, and the stool and Dani were separated, but more fringes bit the dust "—it's true enough," Fred said, righting the stool. "But he doesn't usually go around advertising the fact. He likes to keep his past *in* the past." He eyed her curiously. "What else did he tell you?"

"Nothing much. But doesn't it make you feel strange, calling him boss?" she asked again. "You knew him when he was 'Clint.'"

"He was never 'Clint,'" Fred answered, putting the roast beef into the refrigerator.

"What did you call him?" she wanted to know.

"You ask too many questions," Fred said curtly, turning his attention to the plates that had to be loaded into the dishwasher.

When he turned, she was gone. He smiled then, shaking his head. He had a feeling that this one was going to make a difference to Clint, and he wasn't sure whether or not he approved. He knew of the vulnerability beneath Clint's polished exterior.

"Here."

It was Fred's turn to be startled, but he hid it well. Dani was back, holding the two wineglasses in her hands. "You forgot these," she said, handing them to him.

Grudgingly, Fred took the glasses. After carefully setting them on the dishwasher rack, he flipped the door closed. He took an unusually long time selecting the buttons to press. Dani shrugged her shoulders and began to leave the room. It was obvious that Fred was through talking for the night.

"Master Clint."

"What?" Dani asked, turning around.

"I called him Master Clint."

Dani giggled.

"What's so funny?" he demanded, turning around to face her.

"I can't imagine a big man like you squatting down and calling some little kid 'Master.'"

"Goes with the territory," he informed her stiffly.

She had done it again, she thought in despair. "Oh, wait, I didn't mean to insult you. And there you go again, frowning," she noted impatiently. "Fred, I don't *like* people frowning at me. It makes me feel guilty, like I've done something."

"Good."

She put her hand on his thick arm, preventing him from turning away from her. "Not good," she said. "I don't sing well when I feel guilty."

Fred looked down at her slim fingers, and Dani self-consciously removed her hand. Then he raised his gaze to her eyes. They looked totally devoid of guile. Maybe Clint was right after all, he thought. Maybe there was something to this Annie Oakley creature. "Missy, you had better learn how to sing when you feel guilty, when you feel depressed and when your whole life is crumbling around you. If you can't, get out of the business now. There's very little glamor to this good life they keep touting. Most of it is hard work, tears and more hard work."

She raised her head high, holding his gaze. He could almost *see* her pride rising in her eyes. "I'm not in it for the glamor," she said, her voice suddenly taking on a maturity that had been missing before. "I've gone on singing during an arm-wrestling contest. I've been heckled. I've had men in the audience offer to help me off with my clothes so I would be more 'comfortable' under the hot spotlight. I've gone on after my manager stole everything I had. I *still* want to sing."

For a moment silence reigned in the huge white room as Fred studied Dani. She fought hard to keep her lower lip from trembling.

"C'mon," Fred said quietly. "I'll take you to your room." Under the circumstances, it was the kindest thing he could have done.

Dani walked behind Fred, following him to the foyer. He led the way up the plushly carpeted staircase to the second floor. A luxurious tapestry hung against the wall on the landing. A powerful-looking knight in blue armor rode across a field of white, challenging a ferocious-looking dragon. In the background, leaning out of a tower window, was a princess, also dressed in blue. Dani took an immediate liking to the tapestry and felt a kinship with the princess. The dragon reminded her, at the moment, of Fred. The knight was Clint. Of course.

"Like it?" Fred asked.

She could have sworn that his voice had softened just a bit. She nodded. "Very much."

"It was the first thing the boss bought for the house," he said, leading her to the first bedroom on the right.

A romantic. Just like her. She stifled the other thoughts that tried to follow on the heels of that one. Weaving fantasies would do her absolutely no good. Hadn't she learned her lesson?

Dani wasn't prepared for the bedroom. The word "splendid" seemed completely inadequate to describe the room before her. It was done in shades of wine and fairly breathed femininity. A queen-sized canopy bed, lightly veiled behind filmy curtains, beckoned to her tired body. It looked like something out of the genteel Victorian age. A white chaise longue, covered in a tiny violet print, stood in one corner. On the other side of the room was a long closet. It was mirrored, so the huge room appeared to be twice its actual size. The last three clubs she had played could each have fit in here with room to spare.

"The bath is right through there," Fred said, nodding at the arched passageway. Dani looked in that direction and saw the kind of bathroom that she had thought existed only in movies. The bathroom, its deep red tile glistening invitingly, was bigger than her room at the motel had been. A sunken tub rested next to a clear glass shower stall, offering a choice between sensual opulence and speed. Dani could envision herself there, lounging beneath a blanket of suds.

As if he had read her mind, Fred walked past her and opened one of the cabinets beneath the twin sinks. He handed her a tall bottle that was almost full. "Bubble bath," he said, answering her inquiring gaze.

"Anyone else live here?" she asked, looking at the bottle.

"No."

"There's some missing," she said. Licking her lips, she went on. "Did Clint's girlfriend . . . ?" She couldn't bring herself to finish the sentence.

"He likes to anticipate his guests' needs," Fred said simply, leaving her question unanswered. *Was* Clint involved with someone? You don't need to know that, she told herself firmly. You're not getting involved, remember?

But deep inside, she knew it would be impossible not to get involved. Clint was everything she had ever dreamed of in a man.

Meanwhile, Fred was throwing open the windows that flanked the bed. "Fresh air's good for you," he growled. He made it sound like one of the commandments. "Your suitcase is in there." He jerked a thumb at the closet. "Need anything?"

Dani looked around the lush room. "No, I'm sure I have everything, thank you. Will Clint be—"

"He'll be back late," Fred said without letting her finish. "She always keeps him up to all hours. Did that to Reynolds a lot, too. That's probably why Mrs. Reynolds forced the old guy to retire."

She could believe that. Constance Benoit, with her bright, scarlet mouth and vivid, violet eyes, was enough to make any woman jealous. Dani couldn't help wondering what an all-night session with Constance entailed.

"Good night, miss," he said, beginning to close the door.

"Dani," she corrected. "'Miss' sounded horribly impersonal.

"'Danny' is for boys," was the last thing Fred said to her as he closed the door. Still, Fred wondered if this "Dani" were finally the right girl for *his* boy.

5

Dani sat ramrod straight on the wide, cinnamon-colored sofa, trying to pretend that the two men at the other end of the room weren't discussing her. It wasn't easy.

Albert Reynolds cast a scrutinizing look in her direction and gave her a thoughtful half-smile. Dani nodded at the bald man and went back to contemplating her nails. There wasn't much to contemplate. They were all chewed down to the quick. She had thought she had long since passed that stage until yesterday afternoon. Waiting for Clint to appear, she had chewed on her nails nervously. There wasn't much to do while standing in a doorway in San Francisco for three hours except worry and bite one's nails.

She wished she had something to bite now. Did Reynolds have the final say? she wondered, allowing herself one quick look in the man's direction. Was that why Clint had hustled her through breakfast and brought her here so early?

Clint caught Dani's eye and smiled at her. He looked confident enough. That was amazing in itself, Dani thought. Yesterday he had looked highly dubious about her pleas and had come, she was sure, a hairsbreadth away from telling her to go home and forget about being a singer. But then he had gotten that strange look in his eyes when she sang for him, a look that told her he saw something there. That perhaps he believed in her the way she did in herself. The look had still been there this morning as he ushered her out quickly, saying that he was going to introduce her to his partner before getting started.

Dani wondered just what "getting started" meant.

"I'm doing what you always said I should do, Albert," Clint reminded his partner, keeping his voice low. "I'm delegating some of my responsibilities."

"Yes, but I didn't say to delegate them to me." The smaller man pretended to protest, rocking back and forth in his swivel chair. It was a sign that he was thinking. The more he thought, the harder he rocked.

"It's only for about a month. Just until I get things going for her." Clint grinned at the man he had once called Uncle Albert. "You've been semiretired for two years now. It's time to get your feet wet again." He leaned over and gripped the arms of the chair, halting its motion. "You know you're dying to have an excuse to get out of the house on a full-time basis."

Reynolds waved his hand dismissively. "Mildred's got my days all planned through the end of the year," he grumbled. "This retirement business isn't what it's cracked up to be."

"That's what I thought you'd say," Clint said sympathetically, leaning back against the desk. Earlier that morning he had called Albert's doctor and asked if Albert was up to an increased work load. Not only was he up to it, the doctor had said, it would probably give him a new lease on life. The only one who would disapprove, Clint knew, was Mildred. "Peels and Connors will help all they can, but we wouldn't want to ruffle any feathers by making any clients think we were unloading them on assistants. I'm still keeping the more difficult cases. It's just that I want to be able to devote more time to developing Dani's potential."

Reynolds nodded, but his mind wasn't on any of their unduly sensitive clients. It was on Dani. And Clint. He had never seen him quite so taken with a project before. And he had known him, boy and man, for all of his thirty-two years. "This little girl," he said in his high voice, nodding at Dani, "she has talent?"

Clint turned for a moment and watched Dani, who was now entertaining herself by wandering along the back wall, looking at the array of framed pictures that represented only some of the agency's more famous clients. "Yes," he answered softly. "She has talent." Any doubts that he had had yesterday had vanished once she had sung that song for him. Dani was going to be a star. He knew that now.

"Pretty," Reynolds observed. "Sunday school pretty," he elaborated, shaking his head. "I like it, but that doesn't make it these days. Kids her age like singers who dye their hair purple."

"She's not that kind of a singer." Clint looked at her again. An odd feeling washed over him, making him aware of a desire to protect her, to keep her as innocent as when he had found her. "What she has to offer is timeless."

Reynolds began to rock again. "To you, maybe," he acknowledged, watching the younger man closely to confirm his suspicions. "But to an audience?"

"Trust me, Albert," Clint said confidently, walking over to the bar. He was aware that Dani had turned slightly in order to watch him. She was trying to appear nonchalant, but he could detect her wariness just beneath the surface.

Was he going to drink? Dani wondered, watching Clint out of the corner of her eye. At ten in the morning? Was the conversation between the two men going that badly? To her relief, she saw him remove a carton of orange juice from the small built-in refrigerator and pour it. He handed the glass to Reynolds.

"Been taking your medicine?" Clint asked conversationally as Reynolds took the glass.

"Don't start," Reynolds warned, raising his hand to ward off the words. "I get enough of that at home. I'm sixty-eight, not a hundred and sixty-eight. Noah built an ark when he was a hell of a lot older."

"Is there a comparison there that I'm missing?" Clint asked, amused. He perched on the edge of the desk, his arms folded across his chest.

"This business is kind of like a zoo, isn't it?" the older man chuckled. "Except that we've got a lot more than two of everything." He picked up the glass and took a long drink, watching Clint over the rim. "Is she one of a kind?" he asked finally, wanting to hear him say it.

Clint was evasive. "Come and listen to her sing," he invited.

"Okay." Reynolds put the glass down and began to rise.

"In a month," Clint added.

Reynolds sank back down in his chair. "What's the matter with now?"

"Now she's not ready."

"You're expecting her talent to come in the mail?" Reynolds asked curiously.

Clint laughed. "She needs a little redirecting. Up until yesterday, she thought she was a country and western singer."

"And you know better." It wasn't a question. It was a statement. Reynolds knew how his partner operated: on sheer, infallible instinct.

"I know better," Clint echoed firmly.

Reynolds sat very quietly for a moment, pretending to think Clint's proposition over. Clint knew it was just an act. Reynold's chair was hardly moving. Ever since the man's doctor had initially advised him to go into semiretirement because of his failing health, Reynolds had been searching for an excuse to come back. His health had improved on a two-day-a-week work schedule, but his disposition hadn't. He thrived on work. It was the quality of life, not the quantity, he had said to Clint more than once, that made it worth living.

But Clint had conspired with Mildred to keep Reynolds home as much as possible. Of late, however, Clint had been having second thoughts about his part in the conspiracy. A man had the right, he thought, to live his life the way he wanted. Getting Reynolds back into the mainstream was just what the doctor had ordered, Clint thought with a smile. Literally.

And it would afford him the opportunity to devote himself full-time to Dani. She needed to polish her style before he was ready to release her on the world.

He wanted her to succeed.

Dani felt like a prisoner waiting to hear the parole

board's verdict. She wasn't exactly sure what Clint's partner had to do with the matter, but she assumed that the agency didn't take on new clients unless the older man agreed to it. Age had its privileges, she thought.

Clint beckoned to Dani. She drew a deep breath and forced herself to walk over to him at a normal pace, not wanting to appear as anxious as she felt.

"Albert has agreed to take over some of my clients until I can get you started," Clint told her.

Dani assumed that this was normal procedure. She had no idea that agents generally sandwiched in new clients between their existing ones, waiting until that client proved him- or herself before giving them any attention. She nodded and smiled at Reynolds. She was spared from having to make a comment by the buzz of the intercom.

Reynolds glanced down and saw the dancing lights on three of the telephone's lines. "Oh-oh, already it starts." He chuckled, fully enjoying himself. "Go, go, launch your big star," he told Clint, waving a hand at him. "I have real work to do." Gleefully, he picked up the inside line. "Alice, call Mildred and tell her that I *won't* be coming home for lunch."

Clint took Dani's arm and ushered her out of the office. "Shouldn't we say good-bye?" Dani asked.

"He's too busy enjoying himself to hear us," Clint said, holding the outer door open for her.

Alice, the secretary who had been so cold and impersonal only the day before, smiled at Dani as they passed her desk.

"Yesterday," Dani said in a low voice, "I could have gotten frostbite from the look she gave me when I came in."

"Yesterday you didn't have an appointment. It's

75

Alice's job to discourage people from bothering me," he told her as they walked down the long, thickly carpeted hallway.

"Well, she didn't succeed," Dani commented triumphantly, then cast a covert glance at Clint to see if she had overstepped her bounds.

"No," he grinned, "she didn't. You have a lot of determination," he observed. "That's your biggest asset."

"More determination than talent, is that it?" she asked wryly.

The elevator arrived, and they wedged themselves between several people.

"I didn't say that," Clint corrected. "But talent is definitely not enough. The world's greatest singer is probably out there somewhere working in an insurance office, afraid to make a stab at it, afraid of failing."

Dani sighed. "I've had my fill of failing."

Clint felt like squeezing her hand reassuringly, but forced himself not to. The gesture would be too personal. He had to keep his feelings in check. "You haven't failed yet. You've only been struggling. And no wonder," he observed. They reached the ground floor and began to walk quickly to avoid being jostled by the crowd. "You've been stuck with the wrong act."

"You're really sure about that?" she asked as they walked out of the building. It was a bright, sparkling day, the kind of day on which dramatic things happened. It was a day when nothing could go wrong. She hoped.

"Absolutely. And to prove it, we're going to start by getting you some appropriate clothes for your new act."

She quickened her stride to match his as they hurried

back to the waiting limousine. Excitement shimmered through her veins. It was really happening! She had herself an agent! Nothing could stop her now. Without thinking, she linked her arm through his.

Clint saw the sparkle in her eyes and felt that strange tenderness rising in him again. Was he going to end up feeding her to the wolves? he asked himself. Shouldn't someone like Dani be shielded from all the cruelties of this business? No, he had no right to make a choice like that for her. She had come to him, asking for his help. His professional help. She hadn't asked for his feelings to get involved. But somehow they had. He couldn't help himself. But that was his problem, not hers.

Fred laid the morning paper down on the seat next to him and glanced at Clint's face questioningly. Clint nodded. It was just as he thought, Fred told himself. Old Reynolds more than approved of the new arrangement. He knew the man had been chomping at the bit to get back to work full-time. Fred started the car and began to weave through the mid-morning traffic, heading toward an exclusive shop on Rodeo Drive.

"What kind of appropriate clothes?" Dani asked eagerly as she settled back into the seat.

"Something that doesn't have fringes on it," he answered blandly. "Don't worry," he went on without really examining her expression. If he had, he would have realized that there was joy in her eyes, not concern. "I know exactly what I'm doing."

Do you? she thought. Do you know what being here next to you is doing to me?

Why did these strange thoughts keep popping into her head at the oddest moments?

Last night she had marveled at the whimsical quirks

of fate that had arbitrarily sent her to the depths of despair and then raised her to new heights in the space of less than a day. After convincing herself that things were turning around for her, she had spent the remainder of the night wondering what Clint was doing with Constance Benoit until all hours. She knew that he hadn't gotten in until after midnight. She had heard the door next to her own open and close quietly. She had lain awake, thinking about him, with only a wall between them. She had even begun to envision him getting undressed.

Why wasn't she concentrating on what he was proposing to do for her instead of letting her mind wander like this? Romantic fantasies and wishful thinking had gotten her into trouble in the first place. She had trusted Jared completely because she cared for him and truly believed that her affection was returned.

But had she really trusted him? she thought suddenly. They had never made love, although not for lack of trying on Jared's part. Something had kept her from making the most fatal of mistakes. At the time she had thought there was something wrong with her, that she was frigid. Now she was grateful that she hadn't made the ultimate commitment. Dani didn't take that kind of love lightly, and she knew that if she had gone to bed with Jared, something within her would have been irreparably shattered once his deception came to light.

Would Clint, too, ultimately deceive her? she wondered, looking at him guardedly from beneath her wispy bangs. Would he lead her down some romantic garden path, just to leave her emotionally stranded? Not if she didn't let him get close, she told herself. But was it already too late for that?

Too late? She hadn't even known him for twenty-four hours, she reminded herself, trying to be logical. It wouldn't be twenty-four hours until five-thirty this afternoon. But sometimes, she thought, time didn't matter. Her mother had known that she was going to marry her father within the first ten minutes. Maybe it ran in the blood.

Oh, God, was she going to be a fool?

He touched her cheek lightly. She tried not to act as if his very touch ignited something within her. Professional. Think professional.

"You look very pensive," he noted. "I promise you, this will all be painless."

She pushed her bangs out of her eyes. "Okay, what's on the agenda?" she asked gamely.

"A remodeling," he answered.

"What's wrong with me?" she asked, spreading her hands.

He looked at the child-woman face, the simple shirtwaist dress, the innocent, wary, yet strangely trusting eyes. "Not a thing," he said softly. "But a performer has to stand out. You have to knock them dead before you ever open your mouth. That takes props. We're going to get you props," he told her.

Dani looked down at herself, then cast a shy glance in his direction. "Padding?" she whispered, misunderstanding him.

Clint fought hard to keep from laughing out loud. "No, that department seems to be pretty well taken care of," he said tactfully. Indeed, if everything under that dress was real, she had a very pleasing form. What she needed was clothes to set it off, not hide it.

"What, then?"

79

"Proper makeup, hairstyles, clothes. Things like that."

"Oh," she said, contemplating what lay ahead of her. "And you know about all that?"

"I know about all that," he confirmed with a patient smile. "Constance Benoit favors the shop we're going to," he went on to tell her.

She thought of the raven-haired movie queen. Yes, it would be nice to look like that. To be poised and polished and beautiful. Would she appeal to him more if she were? she wondered. Of course she would. That was probably the *only* kind of woman who would appeal to someone with Clint's background and experience.

He laced his fingers through hers and damned any analysis of the action. He did wonder if he was about to do her a disservice by leading her into this high-gloss world that was half-wonderland, half-jungle. He had seen too many people change in this business, too many people who believed their own press releases. Constance Benoit was a case in point. He had never gotten over the suspicion that, had her mother not propelled her into the movies at the age of five, Constance would have lived a very fulfilling life as someone's wife, growing wider with each passing year and being happy about it. Instead, she had been through five husbands and several depressions that had threatened to end her career. Was he engineering Dani's ultimate unhappiness by doing what she had asked him to? Could the innocence he saw in her eyes survive in the grueling world of entertainment? He tried to cite examples for himself and drew a blank.

Stop getting involved, he ordered himself. She's just

a client, no more, no less. You're good at this. Do your job and forget the sermons.

"We're here," Fred said finally. He had parked the car three minutes ago, and no one in the back had moved. Discreetly, he peeked into the mirror. No one was speaking. Or kissing. He felt free to draw their attention to the fact that they had reached their first destination.

Dani peered out and saw a small boutique. Gold lettering demurely proclaimed the name of an international designer. No mannequins graced the window. Probably too tacky, she thought wryly.

Clint got out and extended a hand toward Dani. She was perfectly able to slide out on her own, but she was beginning to like being treated this way.

"This'll take a while, Fred," Clint warned him.

"I'm not going anywhere," Fred said, pulling a novel out of the glove compartment and making himself comfortable.

They stepped inside the small shop. It was done entirely in beige. Billowing beige silk curtains seemed to be everywhere. They made Dani think of a harem. She looked dubious about the kinds of clothes that could be found in a place like this. And then a thought suddenly hit her.

"Shouldn't I be trying to find a place to stay first?" she asked Clint. Without realizing it, she was hanging on to his arm.

"Why?"

"Well, I can't stay at your house forever."

"True," he agreed philosophically. "But for the time being, it seems to be for the best. It saves time, having you at the house. Besides, we have more important things to see to at the moment than where you hang your hat." It all sounded very logical and kept him from admitting to himself that he liked having her close.

"May I help you?" a stately, angular woman in a refined navy dress asked, greeting them politely.

"I would like to see evening gowns and street clothes for the young lady, Michelle."

"Street clothes?" Dani echoed. "But I—"

One look from Clint silenced the protest on her lips. It wasn't an annoyed look, but it was one that told her he wouldn't stand for any arguing in front of a third party. If she had any protests, they were to be tendered at a more private moment.

Dani kept her peace.

"Any particular occasion?" the woman asked, still not moving.

"Auditions." The single word brought a bright, attentive expression to the woman's face.

"Ah. A performer?" she asked, inclining her head toward Dani.

Dani was annoyed that she was being completely ignored and talked around as if she were an inanimate object. "Yes, I am. And I need a wardrobe for my act."

"Which is . . .?" the woman asked. "Do not misunderstand," she was quick to add, sounding a good deal less distant than she had a moment ago. "The more information I have, the better equipped I am to suit your needs."

Dani opened her mouth to answer, but Clint was faster. "She's a singer. Romantic, provocative torch songs."

"Ah! I have just the thing," she said, disappearing behind a flurry of beige fabric.

And she did. Several of them. Dani felt as if she had

just rubbed Aladdin's lamp. Thin, hauntingly statuesque models came out, displaying dresses that invited descriptions like "captivating" and "bewitching." A shimmering Wedgwood blue dress, slit sensually along the left thigh, made Dani's mouth drop open.

"Like it?" Clint asked, leaning in her direction.

"Is it possible to fall in love with a dress?" she whispered back.

"It's possible to fall in love when you least expect it," he answered.

Something in his voice made her look at him, but Clint had turned his head, so she couldn't see the expression on his face. She was reading things into his words, she told herself. She shouldn't get carried away.

Clint nodded his approval of the dress. Michelle jotted a notation down in the small notepad she held.

Five notations later, Dani reached across the arm of the French provincial chair she was sitting in and tugged at Clint's sleeve. "Isn't that enough?" she asked.

"For now," he agreed, rising.

Michelle looked at him quizzically.

"Miss Christopher is getting tired," he explained indulgently. "And she has a long day ahead of her."

Dani wasn't too sure she liked the sound of that.

"Then she won't be staying for a fitting?" the woman asked, waving away another model who had just emerged from behind the curtain.

Mildly curious about the model's outfit, Dani turned around.

"Oh!"

Clint caught the awe in her voice and turned to see what Dani was looking at. "Wait," he called, and the model turned around again.

"I'm sorry," Michelle apologized, hurrying back to

join Dani. "I don't know how this mix-up happened. Jane," she addressed the model, a faint reprimand in her voice, "I said only clothing."

Jane was wearing a flowing peignoir set. The bodice of the faint aqua nightgown was made up of overlapping rose petals. Dani, who owned nothing but practical nightwear, had never seen anything so lovely. The sleek material picked up the soft lighting and shimmered.

"One of those, too," Clint told Michelle, tearing himself away from the hauntingly wistful look on Dani's face.

Dani missed the woman's knowing smile. "But of course," Michelle murmured, adding the item to her list.

As the model disappeared behind the curtain, Dani suddenly came to. "Clint," she whispered, taking hold of his arm, "who's going to pay for all this? It's going to cost a fortune."

"That it will. But it's time you stopped buying bargain basement clothes," he said, casting a disapproving look at her dress.

He was right about her clothes. She had always shopped economically. Money, her father had drummed into her head, was not to be wasted frivolously on clothes. Her earlier training made her balk now.

"Maybe," she agreed grudgingly. "But first I need the money to pay for all this. My van probably cost less than that blue dress."

"I don't doubt it," he agreed, taking out his checkbook. "But don't worry about the cost. That's my department."

She furrowed her brow as she watched him write out a check. "Agents aren't supposed to do that," she said, the hesitation in her voice indicating to him that she wasn't a hundred percent sure about her statement.

"Agents do anything they want to," he answered, his tone mildly reproving as he signed his name with a flourish.

"But . . ."

Agents were just supposed to make calls and set up auditions, weren't they? She admitted that she was new at this, but she couldn't be that wrong. Could she? She looked at him, confusion in her eyes.

He closed his checkbook and tucked it away. "No 'buts.' I can't represent you unless you're presentable. My reputation is at stake."

The way he said it, it made sense. In any event, she didn't really want to argue. The dresses were too beautiful for words. She contented herself with that.

Michelle took both Clint's check and his business card with a smile. "Tomorrow at nine?" she asked.

Dani suddenly realized that the woman was addressing her. "For what?"

"A fitting," Michelle said patiently. For the amount of money these gowns cost, she would be patient with the devil himself. And there *was* a certain charm to the young woman, even though it struck her as a little rustic. She had learned long ago that you *could* make a silk purse out of a sow's ear. All it took was the proper know-how and talent. And this young woman was far from a sow's ear.

"That'll be fine," Clint said, ushering Dani out.

Dani felt as if she had been caught up in a hurricane, and wondered if she would ever get her bearings back.

6

A beauty salon was next.

The room was bustling with activity. Bohemian-looking attendants with bored, disinterested faces and lime-colored smocks waited on women who wanted to look like the current cover of this or that fashion magazine. Booths lined both sides of the huge room, some open, some not.

Anticipation shot through Dani as she tried not to shift from foot to foot while waiting for the receptionist to return.

Dani stole a glance at Clint. Would he like what he saw after this was all over? What did he think of her, anyway? she wondered. Did thoughts of her burst into his brain the way thoughts of him did into hers? Did he find her attractive? No, she chided herself. She was a client, nothing more. He probably didn't pass personal judgments, only professional ones. And he had obviously found her lacking, she thought.

"Who's that?" she asked suddenly, pointed to a thin, blond man in a white T-shirt and snug-fitting jeans. His blond hair had caught her attention first. It fell over his shoulder in a long, thick braid that dipped well down on his chest.

"Gabriel, the latest rage. I'm told he's a wonder with hair," Clint told her absently, wondering what was taking the receptionist so long. One of the attendants had come out and whispered something in the woman's ear just as they had come through the door. She had hurried away to one of the back cubicles before Clint had had a chance to state his business.

Dani tried not to stare. "If he's so good, why's he wearing a braid?" she asked. "It looks awful."

"Surgeons don't operate on themselves?" Clint offered glibly. "Actually, I'm more concerned about seeing to your nails—what there is of them," he said, picking up one hand and examining it critically. "They look like you've been peeling wallpaper with them."

She pulled her hand away self-consciously. "They were fine until I stood in the doorway and waited for you to come down for three hours," she said somewhat defensively.

"You were out there that long?" he asked, surprised. It hadn't occurred to him that she had waited for him. He had just assumed that she had accidentally spotted him and impetuously leaped into his car.

Dani shrugged. "I had no alternative," she said, trying to sound nonchalant about it. "I'd been turned down by agents before," she admitted, looking around the room and trying to sound as if the fact hadn't bothered her. "Jared," she said and Clint noted that the name was painful for her to utter, "and I had gone to several agents in the past eleven months. None of them would even see us. Their secretaries said I needed credentials before their bosses would waste their time listening to me. Yesterday morning, after I found your name in the phone book, I made myself a promise that if I couldn't get you to take me on, I'd go back home."

Clint felt a twinge of pity for what she must have gone through that had left her so desperate. "And would you have?"

Dani considered his question for a moment. She hadn't actually thought very carefully about what her course of action would be if the answer had been negative. "No," she answered truthfully. "I wouldn't have."

He nodded and grinned. Her answer confirmed his suspicions about her. She was a fighter. He'd back a fighter every time. "I didn't think so. That's what I meant about determination. That's going to see you through all this."

She felt warmed by his smile. There wasn't going to be any stopping her now, she thought. Not with him there. She would make it because of him. "That, and you," she added confidentially, looking up into his eyes.

"That and me," he agreed.

It amazed him how heavy that responsibility suddenly felt. It never had before. It had always been a matter of precision for him: fitting the right performer to the right set of circumstances. Making a hesitant director or club owner see the light. He had never felt a personal obligation before. And to someone he hardly knew. Although part of him felt as if he had known her for years. As if he had been waiting for someone like her for years.

He was getting melodramatic, he thought, watching the receptionist finally approach. That was what came of ushering in a new day in the company of Constance Benoit, holding her hand while she had an anxiety attack over her latest film role. She always seemed to make everything twice as big as life. He had often thought she would do well to have a strolling violinist accompany her everywhere, highlighting her more "poignant" statements.

The receptionist looked slightly harried beneath her plastic smile. "I'm sorry," she said, addressing Clint.

With Clint's looks, Dani could see why the woman would totally disregard her. There was something magnetic about him. She wondered how many women had offered themselves to him, and how many he had taken up on their offer.

". . . little emergency," the woman was saying. "Nothing serious. What can I do for you?"

"I'd like a manicure," Dani said, speaking up. Clint tried to hide his smile, but she detected it in the corners of his mouth.

The woman scrutinized Dani's hands. Dani fought the urge to pull them out of sight. "I can see why," the receptionist said, looking down at her roster. "I can give you Angela in an hour. Will there be anything else?" she asked, peering at Dani with knowing eyes.

"As a matter of fact . . ." Clint admitted.

"Knew it," the woman muttered to herself triumphantly.

"I think Albert might have had a point," Clint said to Dani. She stared at him, wondering what Reynolds might have said about her that had anything to do with a beauty salon. "You do look a little too well-scrubbed." Dani wasn't quite sure why that was so bad, but it obviously was.

Clint turned to the receptionist. "We'll need a haircut. Gabriel. And a makeup consultant," he told the woman. "Ephraim."

"I'm afraid that's impossible," the receptionist began loftily, not even scanning the day's schedule, "I really don't think—"

"I'm prepared to pay twice his regular fee," Clint interrupted smoothly.

Magically, things appeared to change. "Why yes," she said brightly. "I do believe that Ephraim will be able to squeeze you in right now."

Dani allowed herself to be led away by an attendant. Although she was perfectly content with the way she looked, she felt that Clint wasn't. And suddenly, above all else, she wanted to be pleasing to him.

She was grateful for the fact that Clint had opted to stay in the booth, watching while Ephraim mixed and matched colors, creating a new and different image that somehow, miraculously, still remained her. A more glamorous Dani, but Dani nonetheless. No amount of makeup could subtract the look of fresh innocence that existed in her eyes. It was a dewy, sensuous innocence that promised fire once it was breached. But the innocence was so compelling that it held the beholder at bay, making him afraid to change what he saw.

As Clint watched Ephraim apply a pink gloss to her slightly pursed lips, he remembered what they had felt like against his own. Soft, like a delicate rose petal. Had she and Jared been lovers? Had she offered him everything she had to give, only to be betrayed, abandoned? How could anyone turn his back on someone like Dani? Her very presence elicited protectiveness from the beholder. And drew out latent desire. That was what he was feeling now, he realized. Desire. He wanted to hold her, to make her smile only for him, to love her as no one ever had before. She was a sorceress—no, more than that, a siren. Someone whose song lured the listener to forget everything else but the song—and the singer.

Sirens, he reminded himself, led sailors to their deaths.

"How's that?" Ephraim asked for the sake of conversation. He already knew, without needing plebian reassurance, that what he had done was perfect. Of course, it had helped to have something good to work with. He was getting rather tired of trying to make madonnas out of women with hanging jowls and skin that reminded him of worn tractor tires.

"Bewitching," Clint said softly.

His voice brought a tingle to Dani's skin. It was a common enough word, and she was sure he probably used it on a regular basis. But no one had ever said that about her before, and she liked it. No, she loved it. Bad word, she immediately admonished. It could lead to trouble. She had to leave love out of this.

When Ephraim was finally satisfied with his work, Gabriel took his turn at her. For several minutes he studied her in silence. Then, without a word, he raised his scissors.

Dani's hand flew protectively to her hair. "I don't want it short," she protested. The look in her eyes pleaded with Clint.

"Neither do I," Clint said softly.

Was he still only looking at her professionally? she wondered. The tone of his voice made her hope otherwise.

"It wouldn't be her if it was," Gabriel said simply.

Maybe he was as good as Clint said he was, Dani thought, slightly relaxing her grip on the armrests.

Gabriel's scissors practically floated through her hair. The few quick snips he made seemed almost insignificant, but when he was finished, he had taken the slightly wild, rough edge away. The result was that she looked like a sultry wood sprite, half mischief, half untapped eroticism. It was a good combination, Clint thought. It fit the music he had in mind for her.

"I didn't know I could look like this," she said, marveling at the change as she looked at herself from all angles.

"I did," Gabriel said matter-of-factly, taking the apron from about her neck and folding it haphazardly over his arm. He left as silently as he had come.

Dani basked in the admiration she saw in Clint's eyes. He *did* like her, she told herself. The thought did a lot to reinforce the feelings that were blossoming within her.

Clint took her hand, helping her out of the chair. He looked down at her nails. "We'd better get these seen to, and fast. Your hands look like they're going down for the third time."

"If you think that's witty," she said tersely, "I'd say it's a good thing you don't handle comedians."

"Getting high-handed already?" he asked drolly. "Doesn't take long, does it?"

"Not high-handed," she answered. "Just observant."

"Just for that, I'll leave you to the manicurist's clutches."

"You're leaving?" she asked. She didn't exactly understand why she should suddenly feel so empty, but she did.

"Just for a few minutes," he told her. "I have an errand to run."

She couldn't picture him running an errand, and contemplated what it might be while a woman named Angela worked diligently over her hands, muttering under her breath every time she came to a rough cuticle.

"You bite your nails?" she asked accusingly as she brought out a long, thin box.

"Just this once," Dani said defensively, feeling as if she were on trial. She was going to have to work on her self-confidence, she told herself. There were too many overbearing people in this business. She was going to have to stop sounding like an apologetic country cousin and learn to talk back. She was sure that Clint admired assertive, sophisticated women, not shrinking violets.

"Well, don't bite these," the woman told her. "They're too expensive."

"These" were a set of artificial nails. Dani stared in amazement as they went on over her own. Her hands now looked delicate, with long, tapering fingers. She wanted to hold them up and admire them, but was afraid that any swift movement would break them. She was still holding her hands stiffly at her sides when Clint returned.

"What's the matter?" he asked.

Gingerly, she held up one hand. She saw a deep smile crease his face. "Much, much better." He moved to take her hand, and she pulled it away. "What the—oh." He suddenly realized her problem. She was so naive that it was absolutely adorable. "They don't come off that easily. Although you can bite them off," he added teasingly.

"Angela already warned me about that," she said grudgingly. "Said they were too expensive to bite."

"They are," he agreed, leading her back to the receptionist.

"How much?" Dani wanted to know.

"Leave the bills up to me," he told her, taking out his checkbook once again.

"I've never had anyone pay for me before. I mean, other than my parents," she said, awkwardly searching for the right words as they walked back to the limousine.

"No one?" he asked. He couldn't imagine how she had come this far without someone sweeping her off her feet and claiming her as his own. Had he lived in her little town, he would have given her things just to see her smile. He realized that that was part of the reason he was going to such great lengths now. His duties as Clint the agent only went so far. The rest of the route had been chosen by Clint the man.

"No, no one." She slid into the back seat, taking comfort in being in familiar surroundings again. Taking comfort in sitting so close to him again. "But I want you to know that I'm going to pay you back."

"Of course," he said, amused. "Next stop, Fred," he said, leaning forward slightly.

Fred acknowledged the instruction with a barely perceptible nod of his head as he turned the ignition key.

"And just because I'm letting you foot the bills right now doesn't mean that . . . well, that . . ."

"That I have any special privileges coming to me?" he said, guessing at what was on her mind.

She wanted to stare down at the carpet, but she knew that her point would be better made if she looked him straight in the eye. At all costs, she didn't want to be duped again, the way she had been by Jared.

"Yes."

The word was not said nearly as forcefully as she had meant it to be.

"Yes I don't, or yes I do?" he teased.

Dani licked her lips. "I don't intend to use anyone to get to where I want to go."

"Very admirable."

"And I don't intend for anyone to use me—for whatever reasons," she finished in a rush. He didn't look like the type to hurt her, to carelessly use her for his own pleasure, but she wanted to make her feelings plain. Then, if something happened between them, he couldn't claim not to have known how she felt.

"Dani," he said quietly, his eyes caressing her gently even though he made no move to touch her, "if anyone used you, it would be for one reason and one reason only. To touch the heavens."

The moment shimmered between them, and despite her little speech, she wanted him to kiss her. She felt an overwhelming desire to commemorate the moment.

It was just the excitement of the day, she told herself, forcing herself to look away. She stared unseeingly out the window, trying to get hold of herself.

"Where are we going now?" she asked in a voice that was slightly shaky.

"To meet your voice coach."

"My voice coach?" she asked, whirling around,

shimmering moments forgotten. "Why do I need a voice coach?"

"Diamonds need to be polished," he said simply. "Did you know that Richard Burton used to enunciate daily in the shower for twenty minutes in order to keep his voice at the exact timbre that made him famous?"

She looked rather skeptical about that.

He put his hand over his heart. "It's true. That's what made him one of the finest actors in the world. As well as one of the cleanest." He winked, then added more seriously, "Musicians practice daily."

She closed her eyes and nodded. He was right. Again. "Sorry, I'm being too touchy," she admitted. "Anything you say is fine."

"Never give blanket approval, Dani," he warned her. "It might get you into trouble."

She saw that his jawline looked slightly tighter than it had a moment before, as if he were exercising extreme control. Dani wondered why. She had no clue to the fact that he was suppressing an urge to crush her against him and feel her mouth on his once more.

Dani flopped onto her bed. She had never felt so exhausted in her life. She had even been too tired to eat more than a few mouthfuls at dinner. When she left the table, she had heard Fred mutter something about people starving in India, but the voice coach had totally drained her and she hardly took notice of Fred's words.

The voice coach *looked* like a charming old man who could have passed for an elf. But looks were deceiving. What Mr. G. Bagetti was was a domineering taskmaster. He kept telling her that she had more to give and she wasn't giving it. Finally, when the endless session was finally over, he told Clint that there was a lot of work ahead of him, but he had no doubt that it would be fruitful.

Dani had thought he was trying to milk Clint for extra money, and said so in the car. Clint listened patiently, but appeared unconvinced. She was to go back tomorrow, after her fitting. Against her own better judgment, she agreed. Now she wondered if it was going to be worth it.

She was cataloguing the pros and cons, lying flat on her back, staring at the off-white ceiling, when someone knocked on her door. She propped herself up on her elbows. "Come in."

Clint came in, carrying a large rectangular box. Dani scrambled upright as he put the box down next to her and sat on the bed.

"I almost forgot to give you this."

The name of the boutique they had visited that morning was embossed across the box. So that was the "errand" he had to run, she thought. Dani opened the box and found the aqua peignoir set inside, nestled amid sheets of beige tissue paper. She looked at Clint questioningly.

"I didn't think you needed a fitting for this," he told her.

She drew the nightgown out with hushed reverence, sliding the material along her cheek. It felt heavenly. Heaven. To touch the heavens. Dani's head jerked up, and she looked at Clint. Was he giving this to her in anticipation of seeing her in it soon? Her throat felt suddenly dry.

"It's lovely," she whispered. "Thank you."

He touched her cheek, rubbing it softly. "Wear it in good health."

He left her holding the nightgown in her hand.

She sighed as she swung her legs to the floor. Things had been a lot simpler a year ago. Then she'd thought she knew where she was going and with whom. Now, she was floating around in Wonderland without a compass. Had the nightgown been a simple gift, with no strings attached? Or did Clint hope to lure her to his bed?

But if he did, why had he just left? She was sure that he had been able to read the look in her eyes, the look that told him that she was more than half in love with him. That despite this crazy career she was trying to launch, she had considered him her knight in shining armor ever since he had come to her rescue at the Wild Turkey.

Did he want her, or didn't he? And what should she do in either case?

She felt confused.

Dani stroked the nightgown lovingly. Unable to resist the temptation to feel the soft material next to her, she put it on and looked at herself in the mirror. The person she saw was alluring. Alluring. What a strange word to use for herself.

Dani stared at the image before her, then bit her lip and made up her mind. Quietly, she slipped out into the hall. There was no sign of Fred. Before her courage failed her, she knocked on the door next to her room.

Clint opened the door on the second tap. His shirt was hanging open, and for a moment, Dani's gaze was drawn to the sight of his lean, muscular chest. The smooth, lightly tanned skin beckoned her touch. With an effort, she raised her eyes to his face.

He looked surprised to see her. Surprise quickly melted into appreciation as he saw how beautiful she looked. But he made no move toward her, exercising a restraint that had taken years to develop.

"May I come in?" she asked hesitantly.

Clint stepped back, out of the way, not quite sure he knew what to make of what was happening.

"I—I thought you might like to see what it looks like out of the box," she said, stumbling for words.

"Beautiful," he said, not looking at the nightgown or the flowing robe that fell so delicately from her shoulders. "Beautiful."

She wasn't quite sure how it happened. Vaguely, somewhere in the back of her mind, she was aware that she was the one who made the first move. When she thought back to it later, she remembered rising on her toes, her hands sliding up along his neck until her fingers were tangled in his thick, silky hair.

Startled, Clint had not resisted.

One kiss followed another, like the first drops of a spring rain that promised a torrent. Dani felt as if she were being washed away. She told herself that she hadn't meant for this to happen. And yet at the same time she realized that all day she had felt the crying need to be kissed by him again.

She felt the heat of his body as it transmitted itself to her. He held her close to him, his arms cradling her against the perils of the outside world. Their hips met, touching lightly, and Dani ached with an unfulfilled, unexplored need. She could feel every taut, hard muscle of his body, his desire for her as evident as hers for him.

For a wild, abandoned moment, she felt the power of his need as he kept her a tender prisoner against his body, drinking the offered sweetness from her mouth.

His hands slipped beneath the silken fabric of her nightgown, seeking her burning flesh.

Dani heard a gasp and realized that it was her own as she felt his fingers explore the sensitive skin of her breast. His touch was tender, but she felt his restrained urgency.

Now he took the lead, his lips leaving hers to explore her throat, her jaw, her ear, savoring every delicate plane of her face before returning to her mouth once again.

This was crazy. She had told herself over and over that she wasn't going to let her emotions run away with her and yet, here she was. She had even instigated it herself. She was asking for trouble. Hadn't Jared been enough?

No, Jared hadn't been anything, she suddenly realized. What she had felt for him was a juvenile infatuation. Hero worship. That was all it had been, as empty as a teenager's adulation for a faraway idol. That was why she had held back when he had tried to lure her into his bed.

Clint knew that he had to have her. The savage need raked through his body like fire as he caressed her. He suppressed the desire to tear off the delicate fabric and pull her soft, nude flesh against his own. She felt so supple, so pliant. But her look of innocence held him back. Could he rob her of that? Could he put his own desires ahead of hers? She probably had no idea what she was doing to him.

Abruptly, she felt him gently return her bodice to its original position, carefully covering her. She stared at him in confused wonder as he drew back.

Drawing a deep, ragged breath, Clint put both hands

on her shoulders, more to hold himself steady than to restrain her.

"I think you had better go back to your room, Dani," he said quietly, "before something happens that one of us might regret."

Meaning him, she thought.

It took everything she had to hold her head erect and not flee the room. "Thank you for the gift," she said crisply, then turned and left.

Hot, confused, self-deprecating tears spilled from her eyes as she closed the door behind her.

7

She wanted to avoid him. Since that was impossible, she pretended that the incident between them never happened. She made plans to get her own apartment the first chance she had. Feeling the way she did about him, it was agony to have him just a room away and know that he didn't return her affections.

At breakfast the next morning she was chipper and full of spirited plans for her career. Her nonstop chatter was so cheerful that Fred cast a questioning eye toward Clint, wondering what had happened to bring about such a monsoon of words.

Clint felt uncomfortable under Fred's scrutiny, and it showed. Whether that meant that he had taken her to bed and was sorry, or *hadn't* taken her to bed and was sorry, Fred wasn't sure. But he figured the truth would come out by and by.

"Where's the newspaper?" Dani asked, carefully refolding her napkin on her lap.

"Fred hasn't brought it in yet," Clint answered; then something in her self-conscious action caught his attention. "Why?"

"Well, I have to be looking for a place to stay. . . ." The cheerful note in her voice rang a little hollow even in her ears. She pinched the napkin, pleating and repleating it nervously.

"You have a place to stay." Last night was bothering her. It had bothered him, as well. He had lain awake most of the night, thinking about what she would have felt like in his bed, her body curling into his as sleep overtook her. It had taken a long time for his passion to bow to his good sense. He couldn't afford to get involved. It had never worked out for his father, and it wouldn't for him. Not with someone whose goals included stardom.

"I mean a place of my own."

"You haven't got enough money to get an apartment," he pointed out calmly.

"I'll get a job," she said defensively. "Plenty of people hold down a job while trying to get their real careers going."

"No," he said flatly. He couldn't let her leave, even though it would probably be for the best.

Dani bristled. "I can't keep accepting your charity. I—"

He placed his hand over hers, and the pressure startled her. "It's not charity, and it's the most sensible arrangement for the moment. I need you close by. There are too many details to see to," he added quickly. Had she heard the tremor in the word "need"?

he wondered. "I'll see you later. I've got an appointment."

"Arrangement," she thought, watching him go. Business, nothing more. She was going to have to come to terms with that. He was far more sensible than she was.

The ache in her throat made it difficult to swallow.

When she greeted Fred later, outside the house, she heard herself beginning to babble, as if she hadn't a care in the world.

"If you keep on talking that way, you'll wear your throat out before your first audition," Fred commented dryly, assisting Dani into the limousine. Her fitting was scheduled for nine.

Dani understood Fred's knowing look. The stream of words abruptly dried up.

Fred wasn't sure if he liked the quiet any better. He glanced at her in the rearview mirror. She sat alone in the back seat.

Dani pursed her lips thoughtfully, then looked up and saw Fred studying her. "Fred, what's wrong with me?"

Fred's eyes went back on the road. "I don't know you well enough to catalogue your vices," he answered gruffly. His curiosity about last night grew and got the better of him. "Why?"

She shrugged, looking out the window. "I don't know. . . ." Her voice trailed off.

Why had she said anything? She should just let the matter die. You flung yourself at the man and he blocked the pass, she told herself. He kissed you because you struck a biological chord, and then his mind thought better of it. Be grateful. He rescued you from making a fool of yourself, from doing exactly what

104

you didn't want to do. No more getting involved! she warned herself sternly.

It wasn't working. Oh, why hadn't she leaped into Reynolds's car instead? He at least *looked* like an agent. Clint kept reminding her of that knight in the tapestry. A chaste knight, like Sir Galahad. Well, maybe not so chaste, just not, obviously, moved by her.

Fred couldn't take the pained look in her eyes, even reflected in his small mirror. "If it's about Clint . . ." he began, bringing her mind back to the present.

"No, of course not," she said too quickly.

"Well, if it *were* about Clint," he continued gruffly, letting her know that he saw right through her, but for the sake of argument, was letting it ride, "I wouldn't get my hopes up. He's one of those smart men who doesn't trust women very much." He let her digest that for a moment. Even in the rearview mirror, he saw the fighting spirit rise in her eyes. He fought down a smile of admiration.

"He saw his father go through three painful, messy divorces," Fred heard himself say in elaboration. She did deserve a sporting chance, he told himself. "Mr. MacPherson had a lot on the ball, but not when it came to women's wiles. He fell for the glamor every time," he said disgustedly. "And all three of his wives, not to mention a score of girlfriends, used him to their advantage. He had a soft heart till the day he died," Fred ended fondly. Abruptly, as if he'd suddenly become aware of his momentary lapse, his tone changed. "The boss swore it would never happen to him. No falling for the razzle-dazzle."

"I wouldn't know a razzle from a dazzle," Dani said.

"And you *are* trying to get into the business," Fred said significantly.

For God's sake, did Clint think she was just coming on to him because she wanted him to make her a star? The thought left her speechless. She had always thought it worked the other way around, the agent or producer seducing the hopeful would-be performer with promises of fame, fortune and what-have-you. She had never thought of the other side of the coin, had never thought of agents as being afraid of being used.

She sank deeper into the seat, thinking. She was going to have to proceed cautiously.

What was she thinking of? she demanded suddenly. She couldn't be in love with the man. She couldn't afford that, not right now. Granted, his looks were overwhelming, and he *had* been kind to her, kinder than anyone had been in a long, long time. And his kiss . . . His kiss blotted out the world and gave her a feeling of intimacy and warmth like she had never known. But she wasn't in love with the man. She wasn't.

The hell she wasn't.

She might not have convinced herself, but she did her damnedest to convince Clint that what had transpired the night before was a fluke. She had decided that Fred was right. Clint was leery of women who might want to use him to further their careers. Women like a little hick from Idaho. But if she acted as if she could have it all, with or without him, he might not be so wary of her. She was determined to change her image. She began to act more sophisticated, to curb her natural wonder and exuberance. It took a lot out of her, but she managed.

Clint noted the difference in her and grew disturbed. She was changing right before his eyes. Was she becoming just another carbon copy of all the women he had known? No, he couldn't—he *wouldn't*—believe that of her. And yet he feared it was happening.

A week went by. Dani had never worked so hard in her life, both at transforming herself to satisfy Clint's expectations of her as a singer, and at becoming the woman she felt he wanted.

The fittings only lasted two sessions, but her voice coach lasted forever. If she wasn't singing in his studio, she was practicing at home. And then there was the matter of the arranger. Clint had hired someone to revamp a collection of old standards and make them over for Dani, helping her to develop a style all her own. All week long, she only saw Clint for short periods of time. He always seemed to be rushing out somewhere.

She was beginning to feel like a composite of everyone's best efforts, and it was up to her to cement all the various pieces together. Which was going to be tough, she decided as she sat fingering the keyboard in the recreation room, because part of her felt as if she were coming unglued. Was all this worth it?

She slammed her hands down on the keyboard in a display of uncustomary frustration.

"What's the matter?" Clint asked, walking into the recreation room. He had been standing just outside, quietly listening to her sing. Her voice had woven its magic again. He saw the same sultry child-woman who had captured both his imagination and his heart in the first place. This was the way he wanted her to be. This was the way he knew she couldn't—or wouldn't—remain.

Dani jumped. Fred had said that Clint had a meeting and wouldn't be home until late.

Dusk was cloaking the room in darkness. It had

served to heighten her strangely melancholy mood. She hadn't bothered turning on the light when she came in to practice after dinner. Now she strained to see the look on Clint's face. He looked concerned. Probably worried that he had made a mistake after all, she thought. Well, he hadn't. She was determined to show him that his judgment had been right. If nothing else, she still had her faith in herself. She'd always have that.

"Just a little tired," she lied. "Mr. Bagetti kept me an extra half hour today. Said I needed the practice." She flipped the music closed. "You realize, of course, that he's stripping my vocal chords."

"Think you'll live?" he teased.

"I don't know. Hard to tell with stripped vocal chords. I may have to hum the songs from now on."

Clint sat down next to her on the piano bench. She couldn't bring herself to look at his face, so alarmingly close to her own. "Whose piano is this?" she asked suddenly, trying to sound light.

"Mine," he answered, bemused.

"Do you play?"

He smiled, moving his hand slightly from side to side. "A little. One of Dad's clients started out in vaudeville, playing beer barrel polkas. She taught me. That's about all I know," he confessed cheerfully.

She needed to hear something zesty, needed something to break the melancholy mood that was drugging her system like heavy wine. "Play one for me."

"Now?" he asked incredulously.

She looked down at her watch. "I happen to know for a fact that seven-thirty is the best time to play beer barrel polkas. After that, the beer loses its head."

"Okay, wise guy, you asked for it." He poised his

fingers over the keys, staring at them as if the notes were imprinted on the ivory.

"You're stalling," she pointed out in a singsong voice.

"Clinton A. MacPherson never stalls," he informed her. "I'm merely regrouping."

"Oh, is that what you call it now? I call it cold feet." The gleam in her eye was mischievous and utterly irresistible.

"I'll show you cold feet," he returned, taking her up on her dare. "Ready?"

"Ready," she laughed.

After a few false starts he managed to pick out a tune. It was a rousing polka, and after a few chords he began to sing the words. Dani was surprised! He had a pleasing tenor voice. But then, why should that surprise her? she thought. Wasn't everything about him perfect? She had never met anyone so able, so in control of his life.

Control. That was the problem. He was in control of his emotions, and she wasn't in control of hers. Given, of course, she amended as she watched his fingerwork, that he had any emotions to be in control of. It was quite possible that he didn't actually feel anything for her. Jared obviously hadn't, and he had done a lot of talking to the contrary. All Clint had done was kiss her.

The haunting memory of their last kiss clashed violently with the upbeat tempo of the music that was filling the air, and she did her best to banish it. She began singing with him. The result wasn't half bad.

As the strains of the song died away, Dani attempted to maintain the cheerful mood that the music had created. "Say, we're not bad," she laughed.

Unconsciously, she began to pick out the song she had sung for him the first night.

Clint felt the magnetic pull of the melody and fought to keep his feelings under control. "Who taught *you* how to play?" he asked.

"Hmm?" She looked up at him. For a moment her mind was a blank. "What? Oh, my mother," she answered, suddenly realizing what he had asked. "She taught every piano student in American Falls."

"You learned well," he commented. Not everyone could play a song without first seeing the music written down. She was like a magician's magic hat, filled with surprises, he thought. Once again, he wondered about the wisdom of what he was doing.

"My mother didn't think so," Dani said, still staring at the gleaming white keys. She was playing with one hand, the other was propping up her head. "She was always saying I wasn't good enough—kind of like Mr. Bagetti," she said, a sly smile curling her lips as she gave Clint a sideways glance.

He liked her best when she was smiling, although she really hadn't taken on a form that he didn't like. Except when she tried to sound sophisticated. But then, perhaps he was just reading things into her actions. Perhaps he was so leery of getting burned that he wasn't seeing things as they really were.

He curbed an urge to stroke the golden hair that now had beams of moonlight braided through it.

"On the contrary," he told her lightly, "Mr. Bagetti thinks you're a most promising student. He called and told me so this afternoon, after you left."

"Is that why he yells so much?" she asked, letting the melody die beneath her fingers.

"Mr. Bagetti is temperamental. But he's very good at what he does."

"That's what you said about Gabriel," she recalled.

"And I was right."

"And you were right," she acknowledged. The cornflower blue eyes, still bewitching in the dim light, turned toward him. "Are you always right?"

"I try to be," he bantered.

"Doesn't it get tiring, being so perfect?"

He leaned his head back and laughed. "Being right doesn't mean you're perfect."

"But you are," she insisted. Having come so far, she wouldn't retreat, although she wasn't sure where her words were leading her. An anticipatory tingle ran up her spine. "Your judgment is perfect. Your clothes are perfect. Your voice is perfect—"

"—Thank you." He bowed his head slightly, feigning humbleness.

"Your looks—"she dropped her gaze"—are perfect."

She wished she hadn't let her mouth run away with her. She was revealing all her feelings. Why couldn't she just leave well enough alone? Why this maudlin desire to be rebuffed again? She didn't need to be rejected twice in one week.

Three times, she corrected herself, remembering Jared's departure. But somehow Jared no longer counted. Nothing seemed to count but Clint. She felt as if she had been drugged. Someone had robbed her of her exuberance, her desire for a singing career. All she could think of, when she had the energy to think at all, was Clint and what it would be like to be loved by him.

Clint touched her chin lightly and raised her face until their eyes were level. "I've never received a compliment quite like that before," he told her.

"I doubt that," she answered, trying to be flippant. Her voice seemed to be weakening, as if her lungs couldn't get enough oxygen to sustain themselves. "All the women you . . . handle," she said, searching for the right word. "They're not blind."

"No," he agreed, "and they're very free with their words."

There. He thought she was just like the others, offering flowery plaudits in order to get somewhere.

"But their flattery is very empty. It's part of the trade," he told her. There was a sober note in his words. "They say things they don't mean."

"I'm not in the trade yet," she pointed out quietly.

"No," he agreed softly, "you're not."

She felt his kiss on her lips before he actually touched her. When their lips met, she felt as if she had been a prisoner within a windowless, airless box and now the door had been flung open. She felt a radiance fill her as his arms went around her, one hand pressing against the small of her back, holding her to him.

Fitful gasps fought their way from her lungs. A heady sensation overwhelmed her as his mouth moved over hers in a kiss that was both urgent and tender at the same time.

Her body took over, freeing her of any inhibitions, any shackles forged by caution. It allowed her to return the urgency in his kiss with her own. Passion sizzled in her veins, seeking an outlet. She wound her arms about his neck, pressing her throbbing breasts against his chest. One of the straps that held up her skirt became tangled on the button of his vest.

"You're caught," Clint said, pulling back slightly.

"Yes," she answered softly, "I am." I am. I love you, Clint. Can't you see that in my eyes? Can't you feel it?

He released the strap, then eased it off her shoulder,

his eyes holding hers. Dani shivered as if he had removed every last shred of clothing from her body.

Everything within Clint told him to call a halt to this now, before he became irrevocably involved. One taste of her lips had been like a narcotic, urging him on to take another. And another. But that had not been enough; now his body craved hers. He knew this would be no simple merging of two bodies, momentarily enflamed by natural biological urges. There was more at stake here than satisfying physical demand. He felt a tenderness toward her that, left to its own devices, could easily flower into something far greater, something he wasn't so sure he could handle. And what would it be nurtured on? She wanted a career. She had come to him, practically demanding it based on sheer grit alone. It was his job to open doors for her. Doors that would lead her into a flashy, surface world where feelings and tenderness had no place. She would become as empty and as plastic as all the others.

And where would that leave him?

But the rosy shine of her lips, still carrying the blurred imprint of his ardent kiss, was too overpowering. He let his instincts take over.

His hands cupping her face, he brought it to his own. This time there was nothing to restrain them. The kiss grew in intensity with the tumultuous emotion that it roused in Dani.

Her own responses would have shocked her had she been clear-headed enough to realize how different she was now from the woman she had been before he had entered the room.

Over and over again, his lips met hers, each contact making Dani wilder and more fervid than before. It was almost as if she had become crazed. Crazed with delight and fear—fear that the moment would end again, just as it had before, with Clint withdrawing from her. This time she wouldn't be able to handle it. This time, she was sure, she would die.

Slowly he rose, bringing her to her feet with him. She felt herself being lifted gently into the air, then settled back into the strong, protective grip of his arms. Never once did his lips leave hers, a contact with heaven. Her heaven.

He carried her out of the room and into his. As if conspiring with them, Fred was nowhere to be seen, or heard. They were alone. All alone in a world where nothing existed except their need for one another. And the love she felt for him.

He set her down on the floor beside his bed, and she stood waiting. Her breasts, hidden beneath an intriguing blue silk blouse, heaved erotically as she tried to catch her breath. Wordlessly, he reached out to stroke them, leaving them safe behind their blue barrier. He didn't want to frighten her with what he was feeling. Already the strength of his emotions frightened him. Despite the passion he had tasted on her lips, she was still the innocent, naive woman-child who had first captured his attention. He was willing to hold his desires at bay and deal with his own devil rather than hurt her, rather than rob her of her innocence.

Dani moaned, arching into his cupped hands. Pleasure filled her. She leaned her head back, inviting his lips to rest on the tempting white skin of her neck. He took her up on her silent invitation, his lips branding her. She buried her fingers in his hair, pressing him close, arching her insistent body against his. She had never felt a need this strong before, never understood that love could go beyond a two-dimensional level that included vaguely stirring kisses and sweet affections. This hurt. Really hurt. The fire that burned within her did not warm her, it consumed her, destroying her sanity.

"Love me," she whispered hoarsely. If she'd had any presence of mind, she would have been embarrassed about being so blatant, so unrestrained. But embarrassment had no place in the fiery inferno that had engulfed her.

She felt the buttons of her blouse part, revealing to Clint's gaze full breasts that strained for his touch, for the feel of his mouth upon them. Without ever having experienced it, her body knew exactly what it wanted.

Her teeth sank into her lower lip as Clint pushed her back on the bed, his tongue caressing the small, tight bud of one nipple. Movements born of centuries-old instincts made her hips sway beneath him. She felt his need for her grow, and it nearly drove her out of her mind.

Holding her like a precious vessel, Clint slipped the blouse from her shoulders, following the material's path with his lips. Kisses burned her everywhere, covering her aching body, replacing the clothes she wore with a gown of passion.

When she opened her eyes, there was wonder in them. "What is it?" he asked, afraid he had frightened her with the extent of his desire.

"Is it always like this?" she asked in a whisper, running her hand almost timidly along the hard ridges of his muscular chest. Somehow she must have unbuttoned his shirt in her frenzy. She lay cradled in his arms, her body nestled against his, the heat of his near-naked form mingling with hers.

"Like what, darling?" he coaxed, smoothing back

her hair from her face. He hadn't bothered to turn on the lights, and moonlight set her face and form aglow.

"Like fireworks . . . stars bursting inside . . ." Her voice trailed off as embarrassment at her own inexperience silenced her.

The truth came to him like a lightning bolt. "Hasn't anyone loved you before?" he asked.

She shook her head silently from side to side, watching his face. Would he turn from her now that she had admitted the truth? Would he lead her to the brink of paradise, only to leave her in a skiff of paper, to sail on alone?

"Oh, darling, darling," he murmured against her mouth. "It gets better," he promised.

She didn't think that was possible.

But it was.

He held himself back as long as he could, but Dani's demands, as well as his own, rose to a fever pitch until he allowed his own body to lean subtly against her thighs to part them. Over and over, he kissed her lips, her neck, her eyes, drowning her in desire until the appropriate moment.

Unable to keep himself from her any longer, he quickly stripped and entered her. He made the movement as gentle as possible. He kept his own ardor under control and watched her face for any signs of pain.

A stifled moan escaped her lips, but before he could pull himself away, Dani's hands were on his face, dragging him into her hungry, startled kiss.

His movements changed from restraint to the rhythm of spiraling passion, and their bodies swayed to an ages-old tune that was as new as the dew that was gently settling on the grass beyond their window.

They fit together like two pieces of a whole, and

together they went in search of the final peak of paradise. When they reached it, Dani was overcome by a white hot sensation that made her cry out loud in wonder and joy. The long, deep, satisfied breath warmed him. He was drenched with her essence, and he savored the feeling.

She murmured something against his lips.

"What?" He bent his head toward her.

"You were right," she whispered weakly. "About it getting better. Just like I said. Perfect."

He held her close to him, trying to hold on to the moment.

8

When she woke up the next morning, it took Dani a moment to realize where she was. It came to her at the same moment that another fact seeped into her consciousness.

She was alone.

Clutching the sheet to her breast, she sat up and looked hesitantly around Clint's bedroom. Where was he?

Her clothes were all neatly folded and lying on the lounge chair in the corner. She was confused by his absence, and a myriad of emotions dueled for control. Embarrassment won. Dani quickly slid out of bed and hastily clutched her clothes to her. "Some sophisticate," she muttered. "You're acting more like a scared rabbit." Nonetheless, she locked herself in Clint's bathroom and got dressed.

As her fingers fumbled with the buttons on her

blouse, she struggled to get her emotions in order. The sunny aura Clint's lovemaking had created fought with the dark shades of the gloom that had been born of waking up alone. She wasn't exactly experienced in this kind of thing, but she knew that two people who had just shared their first blissful night together and had fallen asleep in each other's arms *should* wake up in the same bed.

Something was wrong.

She opened the medicine cabinet to see if she could find any aspirin for the headache that had suddenly sprung up with ferocious intensity.

"Dani?"

She jumped and hit her head on the open medicine cabinet door. A stifled yelp of pain escaped her lips.

"Dani, are you all right?" Clint asked, rapping softly on the bathroom door.

How should she act? She had never faced a lover the day after. There had never *been* a day after. She had somehow expected the world to look different after she had given herself to a man. To look somehow rosier. Confusion and headaches weren't supposed to play a part.

"Yes," she finally answered, still making no move to open the door.

"Is something wrong?" he persisted.

"No, no," she said, a little too quickly. She was going to have to face him, she told herself, feeling suddenly very nervous. She couldn't very well stay in the bathroom forever.

Running a hand through her tousled hair, she braced herself and threw the door open, nearly hitting Clint.

"Oh, I'm sorry," she cried, jerking the door back.

She looked so flustered and distressed that his heart

went out to her. He had left her sleeping, not trusting himself or his newly stirred emotions. He needed time to put everything into perspective. Last night had been filled with some of the sweetest moments he had ever experienced. During his career, he had encountered women far more experienced than Dani, but none so open, so giving.

Yet he had left her alone this morning, telling himself that he shouldn't have let any of it happen. It made him vulnerable to her, generated feelings that had no place in their relationship. He was leaving himself open to untold pain once her career began to soar. And untried though she was, he knew she would soar. His infallible professional instinct told him so.

It would have been nice, he thought ruefully, if his personal instincts were so infallible. But when it came to emotions, he was as prone to error as the next man. And there were so many invitations to error in this world of glamor. He had seen his father go through too much heartache to venture forth so blindly, yet he had let himself get emotionally entangled anyway. It was time to put an end to it. There was absolutely no future in a relationship with someone who was so career-oriented. The only thing that lay before him was heartache.

Which was why it was necessary to keep a tight rein on his feelings. He'd make no mention of what had happened between them last night. Perhaps, in time, the memory would fade away. He resolved to keep her at arm's length emotionally from now on, and treat her like a distant, kindly friend.

"You . . . um . . . weren't in bed this morning," she said breezily, avoiding his eyes. If she saw rejection there, she was going to shrivel up and die right here on his sable carpet. She had never envisioned death on a sable carpet before, but then, she had never touched the heavens before, either. And she had, last night. She had soared farther than any rocketship ever launched. He had taken her farther than she had thought possible. As she thought of it now, her heart pounded furiously.

"I had several phone calls to make," he answered rather evasively. She wasn't going to make this easy for him. He could hear the hurt in her voice, and he longed to erase it, to take her back to bed and show her just how much he cared for her. But he knew he couldn't. Knew he shouldn't. He hid his discomfort behind a half-smile. "I still have other clients, you know."

Business. Her heart was pounding like a rock star's drum, and he was talking business. Why didn't he say anything about what had happened between them? Had it been so insignificant to him? He had been so tender, acting as if he needed her, loved her. . . . Could she have been so wrong in her judgment?

Of course. Why was she being such an idiot? This had been her first time, but it was his . . . what? Two thousandth? How many women had he sampled in his career? The question made her temples throb even harder. Her headache was getting worse. Involuntarily, her hand flew to her head.

He noticed the gesture and looked concerned. "Headache?"

She nodded, only half hearing him. How was she going to become *the* woman in his life?

"Then we'll have to cancel," he said thoughtfully.

"Cancel? Cancel what?" she asked, confused. The worst ache wasn't in her head, it was in her heart, and she struggled to get it under control.

"The studio, the band and the cameraman."

She held up her hand. "Hold it; you're going too fast for me."

He smiled despite himself. "You should have said that last night."

So, he did admit to the existence of last night. First step in the right direction, she thought with a smile.

"No, I shouldn't," she said, circling the bed, looking for her shoes.

He let her comment drop. Talking about what had happened might lead to other things—which would ultimately lead to problems. "What's the matter?" he asked, watching her search. He didn't see anything out of place.

"My shoes," she answered. "I seem to have misplaced my shoes," she explained lamely, lifting up a corner of the sham.

"In the other room, I think. As I remember it, the lady was shoeless." He hid the smile that went along with the memory.

The lady. He had said the words as if he were talking about someone else. Was that just his way, or was he trying to separate what had happened last night from their normal relationship? Dani knew she couldn't think about it right then as she walked through the hallway and into the recreation room. She didn't trust her emotional state.

There they were, right under the piano. She didn't remember taking them off. Shoes had been the last thing on her mind at that point, she thought ruefully. Dani sat down on the piano bench and slipped on the beige pumps.

"Well, should I?" Clint asked, standing over her. Try

as he might, he couldn't resist looking at her legs as she adjusted the shoes. The memory of her tanned, firm legs wrapped about him made his blood surge.

Dani detected nothing as she looked up at him. "I'll answer that when I know what you're talking about. Do agents always start conversations in the middle?" She stood up next to him.

Kiss me again, she thought, looking at his mouth. Tell me that last night was as wonderful for you as it was for me.

"They do when they get ahead of themselves," he said with a laugh.

"You'd be the only one to do that," she commented dryly, thinking that he was too sharp to let anyone else get ahead of him. "Now, what's up?"

"I hired a studio and a band, and a cameraman to tape you while you're singing."

She was about to leave the room, but at that she stopped. The excitement she should have felt was missing. Everything paled in comparison to what had happened last night. "Why? Isn't there anything good playing on cable?" she cracked.

He laughed, not quite sure how to take her. One moment she was soft and vulnerable, a teardrop to save in a crystal vessel. The next moment she was trying to sound like a hardened sharpy. He knew the latter was an act, but when would it stop being one and become the real Dani?

"Not half as good as you, Dani."

"Oh, so you like my singing now? When have you had time to really listen?" She felt that her best defense at that moment was light banter. She couldn't let him see her disappointment at his blasé attitude.

"I always make time, Dani." He put his arm around her shoulders and guided her into the hall.

Was that what he had been doing last night? Making time? she thought. Well, she was going to find a way to make him change his mind.

"I heard you last night before . . ." His voice trailed off.

What was he going to say? He looked so serious. "Before you began your polka fest?" she suggested, sparing them both an awkward silence.

"You're improving," he said, seeking shelter in a professional observation.

"Told you I was good," she said matter-of-factly, then winked.

For a moment he stopped, and she felt the pressure of his arm increase just a little. "That you are, Dani; that you are."

She turned to look at him, searching his impassive face for a sign of his meaning. There were no clues. "Okay, bring on the crew. I'm ready."

"What about your headache?"

"What headache?" she asked with an engaging grin. "I feel terrific."

He was glad to see the stars back in her eyes, and yet, he wasn't. It was the promise of a career that had put them there, not him. A career was always the center of the universe for the women he worked with. He had no right to expect anything different from Dani. After all, wasn't that why she had come to him in the first place?

"Go put on that blue gown. I want you to look terrific."

She was already at her door. "Who's going to see this tape?" she asked before she went into her room.

"Me, for starters. Other people, if it's good."

She cocked her head confidently, her hair spilling down her shoulder. "It'll be good." It had to be. Once she got her career going, she would be on the same plane as the other women in his life. Maybe then she'd have a fighting chance to win him over.

Clint had never seen her in the gown. On the reed-thin model, it had been a beautiful thing on its own. The model's subtle contours hadn't detracted from it. On Dani, it was like combining two magnificent entities for a greater whole. She was absolutely stunning.

Fred expertly put Clint's feelings into words. "Wow," was all he said as he looked up to see Dani gliding down the spiral staircase.

Dani stopped on the second to the last step, her eyes level with Clint's. "I've always wanted to do that," she said, almost gleefully, reminding him of a young girl. "Come gliding down a long stairway, wearing something gorgeous," she clarified when Clint said nothing. "Don't you like it?" Coming down the last step, she turned slowly around for him. She watched his face for a reaction.

"If he doesn't, his mind's turned to sawdust," Fred told her.

She laughed at the appreciative look on Fred's face. Fred was the last person in the world she would have expected to give her a compliment, left-handed or otherwise.

"You look just the way I thought you would," Clint finally said. "You should do very well in your audition."

"My audition?" Dani asked, stunned. "I thought this

was just a taping so that you could criticize all my wrong moves," she said, walking after him as he went into the foyer. Fred held open the front door for them, waiting.

"It is, but I've lined up an audition for you for next Monday."

Monday. Five days away. Too far, and yet too near. Dani felt butterflies hatching at a monstrous rate.

"That's why I want to get this tape made and study it tonight. More than that, I want you to study it tonight, so that you can get a better feel for what you're doing."

She exhaled through her pursed lips, looking, he thought, like a little girl trying to give life to a balloon. The combination of child-woman was irresistible. No doubt about it, his instincts had been right.

"Let's go," she said gamely, linking her arm through his.

She had expected something along the lines of a recording studio. She had envisioned a collage of wires and equipment, with a microphone dangling overhead. She was surprised to see that the "studio" Clint had reserved looked like a miniature nightclub. A band of well-dressed musicians formed a reassuring semicircle behind her. Clint had demanded that everything be conducted as if she were actually performing in a club.

"Well, at least I get to meet a better caliber of people, hanging around with you," Dani quipped, hiding a sudden case of stagefright.

"Something wrong?" Clint asked, shifting his attention from the cameraman, who had just asked him a question. It amazed him again to see how attuned he seemed to be to her feelings.

"Just a little case of nerves," she said honestly.

"Don't worry; we'll do it over if you like. You're only singing for me."

"That doesn't help any," she answered, taking hold of the cordless microphone a sound technician handed her.

Did he frighten her? he wondered. It had never occurred to him that his opinion, his personal opinion, might mean so much to her.

No matter what else transpired between them, she wanted him never to regret the fact that he had taken her on. Right now her talent was the only thing she felt she had to give him. She squared her shoulders, determination flooding her veins.

"What am I singing, anyway?" she asked. In all the excitement, she had forgotten about her material.

"Just what you've been practicing with Bagetti," Clint said. "Start with 'Love Me,'" he said.

I already have, she thought quietly. She mounted the stage and closed her eyes, composing herself for the routine that lay ahead.

The music rose behind her like a softly billowing sea breeze that grew in intensity. Her own hauntingly sweet tones joined in, and for the next half hour, Dani sang as if she were making love to the audience. And she was. She was baring her soul to Clint through the music he had selected for her.

As she sang the last song, Dani descended from the stage and drifted over toward Clint.

Surprised, he wondered what she was doing. Out of the corner of his eye, he saw the director he had hired waving the cameraman on to follow her movements. And then there was nothing else, nothing but Dani and her song.

And her eyes. They held him prisoner as she sang her song to him, making him feel as if he were the only man in the room. The only one in the world.

> "I don't miss the sun
>   On a rainy day.
> I don't miss a song,
>   After the tune fades away.
> I don't miss promises,
>   That don't come true.
> But most of all,
>   I don't miss you."

Tears shimmered in her voice as she went on singing, giving him her whole heart and soul. Couldn't he see how much she loved him? she wondered. Why couldn't he just accept her the way she was? Why did she have to pretend to be something else in order to capture him? It was the country girl who loved him, not the sophisticated woman who had been created by the combined efforts of experts.

Clint was surprised at how personal the routine felt. He tried to detach himself, and he found he couldn't. That was a good sign, he told himself, as long as it was his professional judgment and not his emotional one. If she could just capture that magic for the audience when she performed in public, she would be a hit. Any day now, Dani would be launched.

The image of a mother bird casting her chick from the nest crossed his mind, and he smiled to himself. Not quite the right analogy. The hormones at work right at this moment had very little to do with any parental instincts. The love he felt was something far different.

Abruptly, he withdrew from his thoughts.

The last number over, Dani bowed her head. Her hair fell like a golden curtain on either side of her face. A pretty picture. The applause made her look up.

"Wonderful." He put his arm around her shoulders and felt her sag slightly. She was drained. She had given her all in this performance. He had been right about her. She was a good performer. Audiences always knew when a singer held back, and there had been no holding back with Dani.

The arm about her shoulders was a professional arm, not the arm of the man who had loved her so expertly last night. She could sense the difference, and it marred the joy she felt.

"No need for a retake?" she asked, although in her heart she knew there wasn't. She had dug into the depths of her soul and given him the best she had. She had gone deeper than she had ever thought she could. Since last night, she had grown. She *felt* different. Changed.

"Don't act coy, Dani. It doesn't become you," he chided. She was picking up bad traits already.

"No, but praise does," she said cheerfully. "I've had precious little of that. Bagetti hammers at me, Fred grumbles constantly every time I open my mouth, and you—"

"—and I just said you were wonderful," he reminded her.

"Real 'wonderful,' or show business 'wonderful'?" she pressed, her blue eyes meeting his steadily.

"Dani, my father thought I would be better equipped to handle life if I studied several languages. Unfortunately, he failed to include gibberish. Want to run that by me again?" he asked. Over her head, he saw the musicians grinning as they watched the exchange. They all seemed to have taken to her. "You can go now," he said. "Thank you all for coming."

At the dismissal, the men began to leave. "You got a great future, kid," the pianist said, shaking Dani's hand.

Dani wasn't sure if he was addressing her, or her deeply plunging neckline, which revealed soft, pleasing cleavage. His eyes weren't exactly on her face.

"Terrific," another man agreed, lining up behind him.

"There," Clint said, waving a hand at the others. "There's your answer, even if you don't like my 'wonderful,' which, by the way, was a personal 'wonderful,' not a show business 'wonderful,' whatever you meant by that."

Maybe it was the success and the compliments that made her bold. Maybe it was the memory of the way she had felt in his arms. Whatever it was, she suddenly felt giddiness rush through her veins as she caught hold of his arm. "How personal?" she asked, her voice low and seductive.

He shook his head, wondering if she had already caught on to the ploys of calculating females. "Personal enough to be satisfied to be your agent."

Dani dropped his arm, retreating behind a false smile. "Sounds good to me," she said brightly. "Well, do we run home and watch me, or what?"

He could think of nothing he'd like better than to watch her. For the rest of his life. He was treading on dangerous ground, and he knew he had to put some distance between them. "Or what," he answered.

"Now who's talking gibberish?" she asked.

"Can't help it. You're infectious," he told her teasingly.

"And you're working on a cure," she said under her breath, walking away.

"What?" he asked, not hearing her.

She masked her feelings and gave him a bright smile. "Just wondering what 'or what' means."

She knew what she would like it to mean. She would like it to mean an afternoon spent in his arms, loving him the way her whole body ached to do. The fulfillment she had felt last night had faded, to be replaced by a craving she scarcely knew how to cope with. She told herself that her priorities were out of order. Here she was, with a career finally, hopefully, unfolding for her, and all she could think of was the way his body had felt next to hers.

" 'Or what' means that I have a few details to see to," Clint explained, breaking into her thoughts.

"Oh."

She sounded so disappointed that he was quick to add, "And it means dinner out on the town."

"Oh."

This "oh" was definitely a lot more cheerful than its predecessor. Clint couldn't help smiling. "Why don't you go change, and then I'll have Fred drop you off at Bagetti's studio."

"Oh."

This one was a moan.

"I thought that since I did so well, maybe Mr. Bagetti could become a thing of the past," she said hopefully.

"Bagetti has prepared more than his share of singers for performances, and you have an audition to think of, remember? Let's not get overconfident."

"It would be nice to," she said, picking up the garment bag Clint had carried in for her. "Just once."

He kissed the top of her forehead. "Plenty of time for that later," he promised.

"Later" was something that worried her. "Later"

represented the unknown as far as the two of them were concerned, and she didn't want to dwell on it. Instead she concentrated on the promised dinner, thinking right past her session with Bagetti. "I'll just wait in the car," she told him, leaving.

"I have to hand it to you," Fred said, stepping out of the shadows to meet Clint. Since they were alone, his tone was less formal than usual, but Clint scarcely noticed. "I had my doubts when she leaped into the car, but you really picked a winner this time."

"I know."

He said it so strangely that Fred was positive his suspicions about the two of them were confirmed. Clint *had* taken her to his bed. He wondered if Clint's armor was starting to rust away. If anyone could do it, the girl with the soul-melting eyes could. After all, she had gotten *him* to feel protective toward her, hadn't she? No one except Clint had accomplished that feat. And Clint had been a child when it had happened.

Fred went off to join Dani in the limousine, whistling cheerfully.

Clint just stared after him, wondering what had gotten into the man.

9

Dani pulled out one dress after another, trying to find the right thing to wear. There were only a few that she considered suitable: the ones he had bought her. But she remained torn for almost an hour, pressing first one, then another against her body while scrutinizing herself from every conceivable angle.

"You're acting like an idiot. He's not the type to be won over by a dress," she murmured. But still, a man who was used to the likes of Constance Benoit wasn't going to be impressed by Belle Starr. She smiled as she remembered the name he had first called her. Well, Belle Starr was going gunning for Clint MacPherson. And she wasn't about to come back empty-handed. Not if her heart had anything to say in the matter. She marveled at how suddenly things had changed. When she had met him, she had been suspicious of his attitude toward her. She had been prepared never to trust anyone again. And now she would offer him her heart on a platter, if only he'd take it.

Dani finally settled on a princess-style lilac dress that emphasized her small waist. She wanted to draw his attention to it. More than that, she wanted to draw his hands to it, to make him hold her again, not like a distant friend, but like the man who had given her that sample of heaven.

"You're supposed to be concentrating on that audition next Monday, not on making your agent fall in love with you," she reprimanded herself as she picked up the other dresses that were spread delicately across her bed. "You've completely lost your perspective, Dani." She sighed, hanging the dresses in the closet. She was going to have to try to keep her wits about her and make sure that she didn't lose her chance at a career just because she had fallen head over heels for her agent. She knew enough about Clint now to realize that he wouldn't respect a person who compromised her goals. And she wanted his respect, as well as his love.

"Ready?"

The knock on her door scattered her thoughts, blowing them away like dried leaves in the wind. She gave herself one last critical glance in the mirror. Not bad for a hayseed. She grinned. She was unaware of the fact that her grin enhanced her appearance far more than the dress did.

"Ready," she answered, opening the door. Just the sight of him standing there, smiling at her, made her heart leap. Oh, I've got it bad, all right, she thought. And that ain't good. The fragment of a country and western song came to her. Sometimes they wrote very appropriate lines, she told herself as she took Clint's arm.

She had never seen anything like Chinatown before. East and West merged with ease as pagodalike cornices stood side by side with neon signs. Brightly lit display windows beckoned her as they left the Mercedes in a parking lot and made their way through the milling throngs of people. Colorful Oriental garments juxtaposed with various forms of contemporary dress added to the town's rich flavor.

They walked past curio shops that were filled to overflowing with inexpensive articles. The shop owners vied with the street hawkers, who had their wares displayed before them, bazaar fashion, in carts. It all swam before her eyes, and Dani had trouble focusing on anything in particular. It all seemed so wondrous and new. *Everything* seemed wondrous to her as she held Clint's hand.

Clint stopped before the China Trade Building. "There's a restaurant in here that has the best Lobster Cantonese in town," he said, ushering her inside.

"I wouldn't know the best Lobster Cantonese from the worst," she confessed without thinking.

He was about to call for the elevator, and his finger hovered above the button as a thought suddenly hit him. "You don't like Chinese food?" It was his favorite. It hadn't occurred to him that she might not like it.

"I've never had Chinese food," she answered. Damn, she had slipped up again. This being worldly and sophisticated was a hard act to manage. She was going to have to watch her words from now on.

He grinned, pressing the button. "Then I'll be introducing you to something fantastic," he promised.

You already have, she thought, offering him a smile.

The Empress of China Restaurant was on the top floor. As they entered, an aura of tranquility enveloped them. The fast-paced world below was replaced with a sedate, fluid atmosphere. A huge, dimly lit fish tank filled with exotic fish intensified the effect.

"They're beautiful," she murmured softly to Clint just as the maitre d' appeared to escort them to their table.

Clint looked over her head toward the fish. He had been here hundreds of times and had come to regard them in the same fashion he did the carpet and the walls. They were just there. Dani brought back a fresh awareness of things, a delight in life that he had been missing for a long time. He smiled to himself, thinking of all the doors she had unlocked within him in such a short time. She had made him feel, despite all his attempts not to get involved. He had broken his own rule again by taking her out, and yet he couldn't help himself. One more taste and then he would push himself away from her. Just one more taste . . .

The maitre d' led them to Clint's favorite table.

"Oh," Dani breathed, overwhelmed by the view. There was nothing at home like this. The table was situated in the corner of a large bay window, presenting them with a panoramic view of the city, its intense, colorful lights mingling like so many riotous fireflies. It took her breath away, just like Clint did.

"Would you like a drink?" he asked.

She was about to demur, thinking that the view and the man across from her were intoxicating enough for her, but she didn't want him to be constantly struck by her lack of sophistication. What did sophisticated women order to drink? She tried to remember the name of a drink someone had offered her at a party.

"Singapore sling," she said to the demure-looking waitress.

Clint cocked his eyebrow, bemused. "That's potent stuff, you know," he warned with a grin. "Two liquors mixed together. Drink that too fast and it'll dissolve your knees."

"I can look after my knees, thank you," she answered with a smile. Besides, my knees are already dissolved, she thought. They're touching yours under the table.

He ordered a Black Russian, and she asked him what that was before she realized that the question marked her.

"Vodka and Kahlua," he answered as the waitress melted into the darkness.

The smile on Clint's face was indulgent, and Dani shifted in her seat, looking away. Tactical error number two. "You must think I'm horribly inexperienced," she said to her fork.

"Delightfully naive would be the way I'd put it," Clint told her.

"Naive" sounded like some dewy-eyed girl who was sucking her thumb. Dani looked up defensively. "American Falls is a little town. We don't *have* a Chinese restaurant and—" She couldn't find the right words and stopped in mid-sentence. She wasn't carrying this off, she told herself.

"As far as I know, that isn't a capital offense." He slipped his hand over hers. He had warned himself to keep this dinner strictly business, a reward for the hard work she had done. But he couldn't keep himself from touching her, even this lightly. "You haven't sunk in my estimation because you haven't tasted Lobster Cantonese, or don't know what goes into a Black Russian.

Those aren't the kinds of things that see a person through life. And, as far as I can see, you're well equipped to make it through life."

She breathed a silent sigh of relief. She hadn't flubbed it yet. As long as he kept smiling at her like that, she knew she had a chance to get to him. The smile reminded her of the look that had been on his face when she had sung to him that afternoon. She *was* getting to him, she told herself happily. It was only a matter of time.

Their cocktails arrived. Taking care not to offend her, Clint asked if she minded his ordering for them. Dani couldn't get over his sensitivity and nodded. The man was one in a thousand. No, one of a kind, she amended. The competition for a man like this was undoubtedly overwhelming. She was surprised that she wasn't awakened at night by women at the door, pounding to gain admittance.

The image made her grin as she toyed with her drink, twirling the tiny, colorful umbrella in her fingers.

"Something funny?"

Dani shook her head. "Just happy."

"And you've got a right to be," he commented. "From what I saw this morning, you've made a quantum jump." He saw the guarded, confused look on her face and elaborated. "You've vastly improved."

She sniffed at his comment. "I wasn't all that bad," she maintained.

"No, not bad. Granted, those people at that club I saw you at didn't give you an honest chance. But you weren't right for it. You and country music just don't click. But when you sing those ballads . . ." A smile came over his lips. "You're magnificent."

She could have basked in that all evening. All

evening? The look on his face could have lasted her the rest of her life.

Career. He's talking about your career. You're supposed to be happy about *that,* she told herself, not at what you hope is some hidden meaning in his words. If you work it right, a career could last you the rest of your life. His smile is yours right now. Tomorrow, he and it could belong to another client. You're setting yourself up for a fall if you believe anything else.

But Dani had had enough of falling. Failures were a thing of the past. This time, she promised herself, she was going to have it all.

Afraid that he might read her thoughts on her face, Dani looked at the lobster dinner the waitress was placing before her. The tail and claws surrounded a white, peppery-looking mass. "Okay, how do I start?" she asked Clint gamely.

He pointed to the little two-pronged fork that had been set at her elbow. "You use that to get the meat out."

She did as he told her. "Seems like a lot of work for so little," she commented when she had finally pulled the meat free of the tail.

"That's the way of the world." He was grinning at her again, highly amused.

"The world's got a lot more to offer than a little piece of lobster meat." She held it before her on the fork and pretended to regard it with interest. It has you, she thought, sneaking a glance at him.

Her words made him frown slightly. Was she referring to fame and fortune? Had avarice gotten to her already? He knew so many people in his profession who were never satisfied, no matter how much they had. Had the disease struck her so soon?

Dani saw his frown and wondered what she had said to cause it. Trying to outguess him was driving her crazy. She decided just to pay attention to her meal for the time being. She dipped the meat into the white sauce the way he indicated and found that the spicy dish tingled her palate. Her eyes watered a little as she took a sip of her drink.

"Good?" he asked.

"Good," she answered hoarsely.

He had to laugh. Beneath the pose she was trying to strike, she was still an absolute delight. Once again he had doubts about subjecting her to the cruelties of the entertainment business. He should save her now, before it was too late.

He had to curb these protective instincts, he told himself reprovingly. A career was what she wanted, and providing her with one was his job. To hold her back for his own selfish reasons would be unthinkable, also unprofessional. She would be all right. He'd be there to buffer the blows for as long as she needed him—before she turned hard, he thought, feeling strangely empty at the thought. He tried to picture her as one of the jaded citizens of the brassy, glittering entertainment world who clawed and fought for a position at the top. His mouth turned grim.

Dani felt the mood shift again and tried to lighten it. She gave him a blow-by-blow description of her sessions with Bagetti as he led her up and down scales and through musical numbers. She accomplished her purpose. She made Clint laugh.

After dinner, rather than return directly to the car, Dani begged Clint to go for a walk. "I feel like I'm going to explode if I don't move."

So did he, but for an entirely different reason. He had never had this much trouble controlling his feelings before. "All right," he agreed, taking her hand.

Dani pulled him along from one window to another, peering in at the cornucopia of merchandise. The excitement in her eyes took him on a vicarious journey.

At the last shop before they reached the parking lot, Clint bought her a little doll which the merchant assured them was dressed in colorful robes that authentically matched those worn by an ancient empress of China. As they stood by the cash register, Dani looked over to the side and saw a pair of long, ivory earrings.

"Like them?" Clint asked, noticing the way she looked at them.

She nodded.

"We'll take those, too," he told the merchant, whose smile broadened.

"There is a matching necklace," he began.

"Just the earrings," Clint said, cutting him short before he tried to tell them that everything in the store matched the earrings.

The owner nodded his head obediently. "They have a message," he told Dani, lowering his voice, affecting an air of mystery.

"What is it?" Dani asked, taking them in her hand and turning them over. Artful characters gleamed in her hand.

"Never mind," Clint told the merchant in an authoritative voice that she hadn't heard him use before. "I'll let her know when the time is right."

She looked at him curiously, bewildered. "You read Chinese?" she asked. Was there no end to his abilities?

"These are rather common symbols," he answered without elaborating further.

"What do they mean?" she persisted as she followed him along the sidewalk.

"Curiosity killed the cat," he reminded her with a grin as they stopped by the car.

She handed him her packaged doll and put the earrings on, ignoring the jostling crowd. "I'm a woman," she said, "not a cat."

"I know, I know," he murmured, taking her elbow. "Time to get back to work."

"Work?" she cried. She had been hoping he'd take her dancing. "But it's after eight o'clock."

"Ever hear of overtime?"

"Are we really going to work?" she asked, sliding into the front seat of the Mercedes. When he gave Fred the evening off, she had hoped that he meant to take her out on the town. Going out on the town didn't mean coming home by nine.

Clint nodded. "We're going home to watch the tape," he said, starting the car. He waited for a break in traffic before he pulled into the street.

Home. It sounded so right.

Don't get carried away, she admonished herself. He meant his home, not yours, idiot. What's he supposed to call it? The condo?

She fingered one dangling earring thoughtfully, wishing there were a magic spell attached to it. If there were, she'd wish for him to fall in love with her. Or, at the very least, for her to fall out of love with him. One or the other. She couldn't stand being in love by herself. And by now she knew that she was. Hopelessly, completely, for the very first time in her life. Everything that had come before hadn't been able to compare to the agonies she was going through. Or the ecstasy she had experienced.

"Where's all that homespun chatter?" he asked as they drove back to the house.

"Just thinking," she answered vaguely, hoping he didn't ask her about what. She wasn't good at fabricating stories at a moment's notice, and she was afraid that the truth showed in her face. As a mysterious femme fatale, she was a total washout, she thought wryly.

"Worried about the tape?" he guessed. It was only natural. He knew actors who cringed at seeing themselves on the screen. Reality tended to mar the perfection in their minds. "Don't be," he said before she had a chance to grasp gratefully at the excuse he handed her. "It only picks up what's there, and except for a lapse or three, what was there looked pretty good to me."

It had looked wonderful to him, but he was afraid that his objectivity had become flawed, so he left it at that.

She wished he were talking about her, not her performance, but she consoled herself with his praise. It was a good beginning. Once she became an utter knockout, she could successfully compete with the other women in his world and win him over. She promised herself to take extra care with her makeup and employ some of the tips Gabriel had given her. No more little hayseed, she thought confidently.

The video room was small and cozy with a huge overstuffed sofa and chairs arranged in a semicircle around a large screen. Clint kept the lights down to guarantee maximum clarity. He put the tape into the video cassette recorder and flipped the play button.

"Shouldn't we have popcorn or something?" Dani teased, sliding closer to him as he sat down.

He grinned, wondering what she had been like when

she was growing up and wishing he had been there to take her to movies and sit in the last row in the balcony. A symphony of emotions ached to break through his cool exterior.

"Weren't you the lady who threatened to explode on Lobster Cantonese?" he asked.

"Isn't there a saying about Chinese food? Something about being hungry an hour later?"

"That doesn't just go for Chinese food," he murmured.

Her heart jumped; she was sure there was a message there. But before she could think any further, he had assumed a stiffer position, and she knew that he had transformed himself into her oh-so-professional agent again right before her eyes. His attention was directed at her screen image, not at *her*.

She sank back into the cushions and watched, feeling both embarrassed by, and highly pleased with, what she saw. She sounded good. More than that, she sounded and looked just the way she had felt when she was singing those songs. Her empathy with the words was clearly evident.

"Pretty good, huh?" she asked once the tape was over and fizzles of snow were playing on the screen.

"The snow?" he asked, tongue in cheek. "Average variety. Of course, being a native Californian, I wouldn't know all that much about snow. . . ."

She drew her legs under her, doubled up her fist and punched his arm playfully. "You know what I mean. I meant me." She threatened to land another blow to his midriff. "Or do you think I'm average, too?"

"Don't get overconfident, hot stuff," he warned, grabbing her hand. His large hand covered hers with ease. "It'll show. People don't like overconfidence."

The playfulness temporarily abated. "Then I was just average?"

"No," he answered, his mouth inches away from hers. "Never average."

Everything about her invited him to kiss her, and he was only human. She made him feel again. He had begun to despair that perhaps what he had witnessed both while he was growing up and after he had assumed his father's position in the agency had robbed him of the ability to share in a lasting emotional relationship. Because of who and what he was, he had never had to make the first move. There had always been women for the taking, and at first it had been a game. But the women were shallow, driven by motives that had nothing to do with him as a person. He was either worn like a decoration, seen as someone to be photographed with or, more importantly, looked at as someone to help them on their way. He had viewed it all philosophically, separating himself expertly from his feelings until he had completely lost contact with them.

Dani reminded him that he was a man, with a man's needs and desires. A man who sought love. He dragged her toward him, holding her tightly, as if he were afraid that she would vanish if he didn't.

Her lips felt like soft flower petals against his. Coaxing them open, he tasted the nectar that was shimmering within her mouth, drank deeply and wanted more. She awoke all his senses and made them cry out for her sweetness. The feel and smell of her drove him on.

Dani felt tears of joy and wonder straining against her eyelids. He wanted her again, her heart sang. Somehow, without knowing how, she had broken through the barrier again. Later she would try to analyze her steps in order to recreate them; right now, she had no time to think. She felt her heart pounding everywhere: in her throat; in the spot his lips were exploring near her ear; in her stomach; in her temples. Everywhere. She held her hair up, away from her neck, urging him on as her breathing grew more and more shallow. Mr. Bagetti would have thrown his hands up in despair, she thought suddenly, the giddy notion flashing through her mind and disappearing.

Clint shifted, and Dani laced her fingers together behind his head, pressing him against her breast, savoring the havoc his tongue was creating as he kissed her through the delicate fabric of her dress. Moistly he encircled her nipples, making them grow and harden.

"There's nothing average about you," she heard him say, and she prayed that he meant it, if only during the heat of the moment. Later she would make him believe it had been true all the time.

"I rise to my surroundings," she said, a warm smile on her lips. She let him ease her out of the dress that had taken her so long to choose.

"So do I," he said with a grin. The elusive, mischievous twinkle was back in his eyes.

She made him feel like a boy and a man by turns. She was a total wonder to him, and he tried not to think of what he might ultimately be doing to her by helping her with her career. Right now the demands of his body were too strong to let him dwell on what might happen tomorrow.

"Touch me, Dani," he said softly. "Please."

Dani felt as if she were a house of cards and he had just blown on the bottom card. Everything inside her tumbled into a shaky mass as she reached out. With hands that were faintly trembling, she opened his shirt.

Long fingers touched his hot skin, exciting them both.
He winced slightly.

"What's the matter? Did I do that wrong?" she asked,
suddenly afraid. She was striving to be as sophisticated
as the women he knew. Otherwise his request would
have sent her fleeing, even though they had once made
love.

"Nails," he murmured.

Her eyes crinkled at the corners as she let her face
relax in a smile. "That's your own fault. You were the
one who wanted me to have nails like a vampire."

He took her hand and brought it to his lips, kissing
each finger in turn. "Not like a vampire. Vampires feed
on others. You don't—" he kissed her upturned palm
"—do that." The kisses, small, light, sent shivers
through her, and this time she made no effort to hide
them.

He brought her hand back to his chest, pressing it
there. "Never leave anything half-finished, Dani."

"Isn't there another show business adage that says
'Always leave them wanting more'?" she bantered
back, her voice husky, refusing to play along.

"I do want more," he whispered. "You learn fast."
He hoped not too fast. Let her stay this lovely innocent
for a while, he thought.

With his help, Dani first removed his jacket, then slid
off his opened shirt, completely unmindful that she was
sitting in just the barest shred of underwear herself.

She pressed her lips together, looking down at his
trousers. He saw a flash of hesitation in her eyes and
loved the display of refreshing modesty, even while he
fought to control his mounting frustration. Rising, he
shed the trousers slowly. He saw desire burn in her
eyes.

Dani rose to her feet, her body almost touching his. She was so close that she could feel the heat radiating from his skin. Within moments she was in his arms.

She took care not to sink her nails into him as she felt her passion heightening. "These nails are a definite problem," she said, curling her fingertips under as she wrapped her arms around his neck. "I feel like I should be wearing mittens to keep from hurting you."

"You're worth a few scratches," he told her, kissing her again.

Dani's knees gave way, buckling as she was pressed backward into the recesses of the sofa. She felt the length of his body against hers, felt his excitement and responded with her own.

Clint's hand slipped from her shoulder, trailed along the soft outline of her body and came to rest momentarily on her leg. Then, with slow, deliberate motions, he massaged her inner thighs until they parted to give him access to the valley that yearned for him.

"Show me," she whispered against his mouth, her words breathless, her plans of sophistication all evaporated. "Show me how to please you."

"Dani, you don't need lessons," he answered with an effort, his heart overflowing. Didn't she see what she was doing to him? Didn't she know that the very scent of her hair, the shimmer of her skin, drove him almost beyond the brink of sanity? "No skillful tricks could have ever made me feel this way," he said, kissing the corners of her lips before he finally drew her into a powerful, hungry kiss.

As he removed the last of her clothing she gripped his shoulders, no longer concerned about scratching his tanned, perfect skin. She felt herself being pulled into a whirlpool of sensations as Clint rocked her against him.

Suddenly their positions were reversed and she found herself looking down into his face. His expression, so odd, was one she couldn't understand. Traces of pain were in his eyes. Had her nails hurt him again?

"What?" she asked, wanting to ease whatever it was that hurt him.

"Shh." He threaded his fingers through the golden veil that hung down about her, lightly tickling his chest, and drew her face to his. "There's a time when words should be stilled," he told her, his voice barely a whisper. "Even yours."

His kiss sent desire hurtling through her veins, and time vanished. With no prompting from him, she knew when he was ready, when they were both ready. She arched to admit him, glorying in the feeling that filled her.

And when it was over, that was wonderful, too. She curled like a contented kitten against him, reveling in the male smells that rose up against her cheek as she pressed it to his chest. If she had to die, she would pick this time, this place. She had never been happier.

10

•-00000000000-

Dani didn't see Clint the entire next day. Once again she couldn't escape the feeling that he was avoiding her. He had taken the Mercedes and let Fred ferry her to Bagetti's studio. She had no way of knowing that he was running from himself more than he was from her.

"It's like being in love with Zorro," she muttered. "He carves a 'Z' on my heart and rides off into the night."

"Come, come, if it's important, say it out loud. If not, concentrate on your work," Mr. Bagetti ordered, easily raising his rotund little body up on his toes. For a man who undoubtedly tipped the scales at over two hundred pounds, and carried it all on a five-foot-five body, he moved with surprising agility. Especially when he thought she hit a wrong note. Which, he told her, was often.

Dani sighed, turning her face toward the sun that was

streaming in through the uncurtained window. "It's not important," she replied.

"Good, we'll begin again. And this time, try to look as if it didn't hurt, eh?" He brushed her cheek with his thumb. It was a kindly gesture, and she could see by the look in his eyes that he knew something was troubling her, but wouldn't risk hurting her further by probing. Neither would he let it interfere with her lesson, however. "Mr. MacPherson said the audition is for Monday, right?"

She nodded.

He half closed his lids and shook his head. "Lots of work. Lots of work." He raised his hands in an upward tempo. "Again," he commanded.

Dani frowned. "If I'm really that bad, why are you bothering?"

He wasn't used to being questioned, but he indulged her. "I am being severely critical of you so that others will not be. Makes sense?" He cocked his head, waiting for her assent.

"Yes," she murmured, taking a deep breath.

Her sessions with Bagetti had been doubled, leaving her precious little time for herself, much less to see Clint. He wasn't at dinner that night. And when she stopped him to talk the following day, he seemed in a hurry to leave. She wanted to come right out and ask him if he was trying to avoid her, but she knew that such a question wasn't in keeping with the image she was trying to get across to him. So she bit her lip and made a comment about how hectic his schedule was.

"Agents don't keep regular hours, Dani," Clint told her evasively.

"Kind of like doctors, hmm?"

He laughed, his hand on the doorknob. "Nothing nearly so noble. But I've got a lot of details to see to. You're not my only client," he told her as he left.

She stood in the foyer, feeling very, very alone. "No," she whispered, "I know I'm not."

He hated the look he had seen in her eyes just before he walked out. It made trying to divorce himself emotionally from her all the harder. But he knew it had to be done. He saw how easily she was beginning to fit into the entertainment world. In the end she would be another Barbara Dirken, another Constance Benoit. There was no future for them.

He hurried out to the Mercedes.

"Where's Clint?" she asked Fred as she watched him set only one place for dinner. Again.

"Mrs. Reynolds called him yesterday and put her foot down about Mr. Reynolds's working hours, so the boss is back at it."

"Oh." She looked around the dining room glumly. "I don't think I'm very hungry, Fred."

He whirled around from the door. "Just because he's a workaholic doesn't mean you have to go on a hunger strike," he snapped waspishly. "Harper's going to think he's listening to a real live canary auditioning come Monday." He eyed her, acting disgruntled. "Well, it's your body," he muttered, shaking his head.

Dani could see through his act by now. Still, he did have a point. Not eating wasn't going to make Clint appear. Besides, how was she going to impress Harper and make Clint proud of her if she keeled over at the audition? "Okay," she surrendered, "I'll eat."

"Now you're finally making sense," he snorted.

"But only in the kitchen—with you."

He looked at her for a moment, then waved her forward. "I suppose if I have to, I have to."

It was a lot nicer to sing for Herbert Harper than for Mr. Bagetti. The heavy-set, balding man smiled easily as he sat next to Clint, nodding and listening. Except for Harper and Clint, there was no one else on the floor of the club. One lone musician, a pianist, provided the background music. Dani provided the soul.

She tried to pretend that this was just another practice session. Lord knew she had had a sea of those in the last five days, she thought. Her ploy worked, to an extent. Her pounding heart stayed under control, and all the passion and ardor that had been pent up within her were evident in her voice. If Harper liked her, she would appear in something the club owner called "semi-professional night." Talented, unknown artists were allowed to perform on the same bill as a well-known local attraction. It promised them a good audience and an opportunity to begin their careers.

Dani performed four songs that Clint felt were her best numbers. Once she was finished, she placed the microphone on the piano and walked toward the two men. She was sure of herself, yet she was worried, too. Harper was smiling, but then he had been smiling ever since she had walked into the room. Did it mean anything?

She looked from one man to the other. Clint nodded slightly, and she knew it meant that he was pleased. Well, that was something, at least. But right now Clint's opinion wasn't the one that counted. Harper's was.

"Well, Mr. Harper?" Clint asked expectantly, his voice warm, but prodding. "Isn't she everything I told you she was?"

Slowly, thoughtfully, the freckled, bald head nodded. "And more." Harper rose to his feet, pumping Dani's hand. "Young lady, that was a very fine audition. So fine that I'd like to make you a little proposition. The singer who usually opens for Barbara—that's Barbara Dirken, of course—just called me from the hospital. Seems her appendix picked last night to flare up. That leaves me with a problem."

Dani stared at him. He couldn't be saying what she thought he was saying. Things like that only happened in old movies, didn't they?

"I'd like you to take her place. I've got a temporary act for a couple of days, but nothing like you. You'd start Wednesday, if that's all right with you."

Dani's heart leaped into her throat, making it very difficult for her to speak intelligibly, but somehow she managed. "All right with me? That's wonderful with me! Oh, Mr. Harper, you won't be sorry. You—" She caught herself. She sounded like an enthusiastic child, not like the sophisticated woman she was trying to be. Abruptly, her tone changed. "That would be very nice, Mr. Harper," she said, smiling at him serenely. "I'll let you and Clint make the arrangements." She smiled at Clint. "I'll wait for you in the car." There, wasn't that the way Constance Benoit would have handled it? she thought proudly.

Clint looked at her quizzically. What was going on? She had gone from being excited to sounding as if she were jaded. He frowned.

She noticed the cloud that darkened his eyes and wondered what she had done wrong. Didn't *anything* please him?

"Clint! It's been too, too long!"

Dani swung around to see the owner of the honeyed voice as Barbara Dirken swept into the room, making it hers.

At thirty-three, Barbara Dirken was a legend in her own time. Dani was impressed. Even though she had primarily listened to country and western stations, she knew who Barbara Dirken was. *Everyone* knew who the titian-haired woman was. She had a voice as strong and clear as any singer could hope for. Though she was often grossly temperamental, all was forgiven the small, thin woman whenever she opened her mouth to sing. One reviewer had once said she could elicit tears from a stone if she wanted to. She had made her way from obscurity to the top fifteen years ago, and had persevered while other singers had come and gone. Dani looked at the woman in awe.

Barbara sailed right past her, offering a quick smile to Harper. But it was on Clint that her attention was focused. She opened her arms in an expansive embrace. Dani mused that if it weren't for the fur she had casually draped around her neck, Barbara might have swallowed Clint up. She kissed his cheek and then seemed to nestle into the same space he was occupying, her lithe body fitting neatly against him. Dani watched, waiting for the woman to start cooing and fluttering her lashes.

"Where have you been hiding?" Barbara asked, her eyes shining as they danced over him.

"Just working, Barbara," he said, his voice politely indulgent.

Barbara rested one scarlet fingernail against the top button of his shirt. "That was always your problem, Clint," she purred. "Work, work, work." She looked at

Harper. "Did you know that Clint was my agent, oh, how long has it been now?" she asked, turning toward Clint.

Dani felt something smoldering within her as she watched the woman practically drape herself over Clint.

"Two years," Clint said, answering her question for Harper's benefit.

"Right." Barbara nodded. "Two years since you let me go."

"No one 'let you go,' Barbara," he reminded her tolerantly, remembering how much patience and pampering she had always required from him. "You wanted to go."

"Details, details," she laughed, waving away his words. "I've missed you, you know," she said, her eyes appreciatively taking in the classic features of his face and the slightly gaunt, high cheekbones.

Dani had never experienced such raw, primitive jealousy before. It shocked and surprised her that she suddenly wanted to tear into someone and find out what clumps of curly red hair felt like between her fingertips. She fought hard to maintain the artificial smile on her face.

"Listen, sugar, why don't we have dinner tonight and talk over old times?" Barbara proposed. "I just happen to have a free evening."

"I'm afraid I don't," Clint answered smoothly.

Barbara looked pouty for a moment and then gave up. "Work again?" she asked loftily.

"I've got a few arrangements to see to for Dani," he told her.

She sighed dramatically. "I've been replaced by a boy."

"No one could replace you, Barbara," Clint said,

knowing she liked to hear that sort of flattery. If Dani were going to be working at the Club Horizon, it was better all around if nothing ruffled Barbara's feathers. She could get very nasty when she felt the situation called for it.

Clint put out his hand toward Dani and she came forward. "This is Dani Christopher," he said, introducing her. "She'll be opening for you."

Barbara's wide-set, amber eyes were unsmiling as she looked Dani over carefully, though she kept a frosty smile on her lips. "What happened to Sharon?" she asked Harper.

"Shiela," Harper corrected her, though he mumbled the name into his chin. Dani could see that he was cowed by the woman. "Appendix," he began.

Barbara waved away the rest of the explanation. "Boring little things, appendices. Never had one myself." She accompanied the words with a deep, throaty laugh. A regal hand was extended toward Dani. It was limp and cold. "Hello."

It was a chilly greeting, and Dani had to curb the urge to respond in kind. After all, that wouldn't be in keeping with the sophisticated role she had cast herself in. So she took the offered hand and shook it. "How do you do, Miss Dirken. I'm a great admirer of yours." That sounded right, didn't it? Even if it did stick in her throat.

"Of course you are," Barbara murmured, obviously unimpressed. "Well, I want to talk to you about that cramped little box you call a dressing room, Herbert, so do be quick about your business. I'll be waiting in your office," she told the nervous man. "And, Clint," she said, her eyes speaking volumes, "I haven't given up. Now that I see you again, I don't know how I ever let you get away."

She made a dramatic exit, sauntering off toward the back. It was done for effect. Clint shook his head tolerantly. "Same old Barbara," he commented to Harper.

"She really pulls them in, though," Harper said. "So it's worth any little . . . tempests that might come up. I was lucky to get her."

"Hear that?" Clint asked, turning toward Dani. "You'll be playing to packed crowds."

Dani nodded, too disturbed by Barbara's vague promise about Clint to react one way or the other. Just what had the woman meant by "get away"? Was she just talking, or had there been something between Clint and Barbara? Something that Barbara wanted to resurrect? And if Barbara was serious, just what kind of a chance did Dani herself have against someone as glamorous as Barbara Dirken? The amused look on Clint's face didn't give her a clue.

Well, she wasn't going to mope over it, she told herself. She had an act to get together. Once she felt confident enough about her performance at the club, *then* she'd tackle her other problem. Actions, she knew, spoke louder than words, and being a successful client would speak loudest of all.

She threw herself into her practice sessions with a vengeance, surprising Bagetti by asking for even more time than was allotted to her. The little man looked over toward Fred, who was sitting patiently, reading a book and waiting to take Dani home. Fred appeared to be paying strict attention to his book, but he nodded. Bagetti shrugged his wide shoulders. He was being well paid for his time, and there wasn't another student coming for an hour.

"Very well, let us begin with the third number. It is a little shaky."

So was she, Dani thought, but no one else knew it.

Dani stood outside the Club Horizon on Wednesday morning, looking at the sign announcing that Barbara Dirken was performing there direct from a smash engagement in Las Vegas. In letters that were far smaller, the sign read, "And introducing Danielle Christopher in her San Francisco debut."

Dani smiled. That wasn't quite right. She had played San Francisco before. But the Dani Christopher who had played the Wild Turkey was light-years away from the woman who was going on tonight. Judging from the looks the musicians had given her at the taping last week, she had finally come upon her niche in life. And it had taken Clint to find it for her.

She ran her fingers along the glass, wishing she could touch the sign itself. For luck. But then, what did she need with luck? She had Clint, at least professionally. Things could only go up from here.

Dani walked into the club. The main room was still dusky. It looked gloomy, but not to her. This was going to be the site of the birth of her career. She was, as the old expression went, going to knock them dead. She had every intention of being just as good as Barbara Dirken. After all, why should success only strike once? An electrical charge raced through her.

She felt wonderful.

Dani slowly walked around the white-covered tables, their chairs stacked on top to show that the cleaning crew had been through.

"You're here early."

Dani turned to find Mr. Harper, dressed far more

casually than he had been on Monday, approaching her from the side. He was wearing a loud Hawaiian shirt that seemed in keeping with his cherubic, moon-round face.

"I couldn't keep away," she confessed. There was no point in trying to act sophisticated with a man in a Hawaiian shirt. Besides, she felt uncomfortable about it. The act didn't suit her.

Harper looked down at the sheet music she was clutching. Dani followed his glance. "I thought that I'd run through my numbers a few more times with Eddie, if he didn't mind. He *is* here?" she asked suddenly, realizing that she had gotten ahead of herself again. Fred had left with Clint that morning, assuming that she would busy herself at home with preparations for tonight. On an impulse, she had decided to come in early to practice one more time before the show.

"Just got here," Harper told her. "Been muttering something about the arrangements being strange."

"Clint had someone tailor them to fit," she explained, trying not to apologize for the fact.

Harper nodded in response, only half listening. "I'll find him for you." He retreated backstage in search of the pianist.

She jumped nimbly up on stage. She was wearing jeans and felt relaxed. She loved the glamorous clothes and artful makeup, but putting them on was like putting on a costume to play a part. Underneath it all, she was still the country girl from Idaho. She doubted that would ever change. But she was determined to keep that fact from Clint. For him she would be a prairie flower who had blossomed into a city rose.

Eddie walked out of the back room, clutching a coffee

160

mug that was at least twice as big as anything she had ever seen.

"Like coffee, huh?" she asked.

Eddie's half-opened eyes slid in her direction. His brown sweater and slacks and hooded glance made her think of a slithering snake—harmless, she hoped.

"Can't get my heart going unless I've got a gallon of the stuff in my blood." He set the mug down with a bang on top of the piano and addressed himself to the keyboard, running through a scale to get his fingers nimble. "Harper says you want to practice again." She had been there yesterday with her chauffeur in tow and had sounded pretty good. He was surprised to see her back before noon.

"I want to run through the material a couple of times," she said, pushing her bangs out of her eyes. They kept dipping and hiding her eyes. She had to remember to do something about them for tonight.

"Fine with me," Eddie said, taking a huge gulp of coffee. He began to play the opening bars of the first song and faltered for a moment. "Seems like I'm the one who needs practice, not you," he muttered, starting over again.

She hoped she'd remain that cool if she stumbled. Right now, she felt that she would break apart like a brittle icicle if she made one wrong move.

But there were no wrong moves, no wrong notes. Her voice carried, full of all the emotions she felt. As she heard herself, Dani grew bolder, more confident, and it showed. She was going to be all right tonight. More than that, she told herself, she was going to be terrific.

Out of the corner of her eye she saw Barbara Dirken enter with two men in close attendance. Dani recognized one of them. He had been at the club yesterday, when she was practicing. She offered him a smile and received a curt nod in return. To Dani's surprise, Barbara, her flaming red hair hidden beneath a kelly green turban that matched her form-fitting suit, sat down at the center table. Her face looked grim as she listened to Dani.

Dani felt a nervous knot tightening in her stomach as she went on. Halfway through the next number, Dani saw Barbara lean over and snap something at the man at her side. He left quickly, disappearing off to the side.

What was wrong? Dani wondered, glancing back at Eddie. Eddie seemed oblivious to what was going on, lost in the music. Somehow Dani finished the number. And then she stopped.

"Is there something wrong, Miss Dirken?" she asked, getting off the stage.

"Plenty," the woman spat, rising to her feet. In her heels and turban, she towered several inches above Dani, and Dani felt that the woman was trying to use both her height and her reputation to intimidate. A stubborn look came into Dani's eyes.

"Maybe we can talk about it," Dani offered, devoid of her normal cheerfulness.

"The hell we can," Barbara said, pushing past Dani.

Her companion had brought back a very changed-looking Harper. The cherubic face was lined with concern as he looked nervously from Dani to Barbara. In his hand he clutched a rolled-up collection of papers. "Now, Barbara," he said soothingly, trying to put his hand on her arm.

She shrugged him off as if she were shedding lint. "Don't you 'Now, Barbara' me. What are you trying to pull here?"

Dani stared, utterly bewildered, but knowing that somehow it wasn't going to go well for her.

Harper sighed wearily, trying to maintain a smile that was drooping badly at the corners. "No one's trying to pull anything, Barbara."

"Fine," she snapped. "Then get rid of her."

Dani stood rooted to the spot, stunned. What was the woman saying?

"Calm down, Barbara," Harper pleaded. "Maybe we can work this out." His voice faltered.

"The only way I'm working is if she goes," Barbara said, pointing at Dani. "I came down to tell you that, and now that I've heard her, I'm more determined than ever."

Dani felt her blood beginning to boil. Just who the hell did the woman think she was? Some sort of goddess to be obeyed and scraped before? Well, that definitely wasn't her style.

"I have a name, Miss Dirken," Dani said tersely.

The icy gaze shifted in Dani's direction. "All right, get rid of 'Dani,'" she said, exaggerating the name.

"But I need an opening act," Harper wailed.

"Get a trained chimpanzee. Get anything you want, but don't get anyone who sounds that good!" she shouted, pointing an accusing finger at Dani. "I don't need competition. My God, I've spent years getting rid of my competition." She glared at Dani. "When Clint told me last night that she was a little singer from Idaho who needed a break, I thought she'd sound like someone fresh out of a church choir. Not like . . . like *that*. If it hadn't have been for George, I'd never have known until tonight," she snapped accusingly at Harper. The club owner cringed visibly.

A rushing noise filled Dani's head. Clint had discussed her with Barbara? Why? And last night? He had been avoiding her and availing himself of the affections of this human barracuda!

Barbara seemed to read her mind, and it suited her to twist the knife a little. "Of course, we didn't spend much time talking last night." The smile was malicious.

Dani felt as if she had received a blow to her stomach. She was going to be physically ill in another moment. Her eyes shifted toward Harper, but the man was having his own problems.

"Well, now, maybe I *was* mistaken, Dani," he said slowly, avoiding her eyes. He was talking to the space above her head. "You really don't seem right for this spot. That is . . . I . . . well . . ." His tongue darted over his dry lips as he tried to search for words.

Dani knew that she had had enough.

She looked at the helpless expression on Harper's face. In his hand he was carrying a contract. Her contract. The one she had signed just yesterday. Slowly she walked over to him and took it out of his damp hand.

Staring straight into Barbara's eyes, she methodically tore the contract in half, then threw it on the ground. "Fear can be a terrible thing, Miss Dirken. It can paralyze your vocal chords when you least expect it." And if I could put a curse on you, I'd do it, she added silently.

With that Dani turned and walked out without ever looking back.

11

Dani made up her mind in the cab.

She was going to go home. Her home. She had had enough disappointments and letdowns to last her a lifetime. The bottom had finally dropped out of her world when Barbara had smiled her sly smile and hinted that her evening with Clint had led to a renewal of old intimacies.

Dani had enough money left from the two hundred dollars that Clint had collected for her engagement at the Wild Turkey to pay for a bus ticket. That was all that mattered.

She left the cab waiting for her a short distance from the house, planning to slip out quietly. She wanted to avoid any questions if Fred were home and should see the cab waiting out front. Clint, she knew, wasn't home at all. He was hiding out at work. That was the only way to describe it. Since the last time he had made love to her, she had seen him only a handful of times, always in Fred's company, always politely distant. It would seem, she thought ruefully, fumbling with the key Clint had given her, that he regretted what had happened between them. There was no other explanation for his treatment of her, or for his spending the evening in Barbara's arms while she sat alone, aching for him.

Well, he didn't have to be ashamed or play hide and seek any longer. Soon she'd be gone. Out of his life for good.

The thought left her empty. If she left, she'd never see him again. Ever. She couldn't picture Clint coming to American Falls in search of her. No, if she left, that would definitely be it.

The tenacious side of her balked. She had always dug in and fought for what she wanted before. But that was just the trouble. She was tired of fighting.

Dani tossed the few items she had to call her own into the battered valise she had brought with her an eternity ago. The meter on the cab was running, and she couldn't afford to waste time packing neatly. Or writing a note.

Besides, he'd probably be relieved to find her gone. He hadn't wanted to take her on in the first place. She had forced herself on him. For all she knew, maybe he hadn't wanted to make love to her, either. Maybe she had somehow forced that on him, too. A tear stung her eye. She brushed it aside with the back of her hand. Another sprang up in its wake. She wasn't going to cry. She wasn't, she told herself. She had some dignity left. She was doing the only smart thing. What did she need with a life where conceited vipers could cut her dead and the man she loved stood coldly by?

Coldly. The thought made her stop for a moment.

When they had made love, Clint had been very warm, very tender. . . . Stop it! she told herself. It's all just your imagination. What was he supposed to do at the time, kick you out of bed? You're a novice at this. What happens in bed doesn't count. It's what happens *out* of bed that matters. And what happened out of bed was that he treated her with the same distant politeness that he would treat the man in the street. Well, she had had enough of that! Let him go to Barbara, or Constance, or whomever. She was tired of trying to be something she wasn't. Tired of trying, period.

Dani hurried down the hall. She only paused for a moment as the tapestry caught her eye. She touched the shining fabric lovingly.

"Good-bye," she murmured.

And then she flew down the stairs, pushing her emotions aside and thinking only of the details before her. She'd ask the driver to take her to the nearest bus terminal and get the first bus out to Idaho. From there, she'd make her way back home. If need be, she'd call her family for help. Her brother would come and get her—if it didn't interfere with any of his plans, she added ruefully. No one had time for her in their lives unless there was a lull, she thought, feeling sorry for herself. Another tear fell, and she had trouble seeing the cab.

"Take me to the nearest bus terminal," she said, getting into the cab. "I want to get a bus going to Idaho."

"I only know where they are, I don't know where they go," the man said, pulling away from the curb. "Me, I've never left San Francisco. Got everything I want right at home."

"You're lucky," she muttered, more to herself than to

him. Listlessly she fell back against the vinyl seat. This time she didn't bother wiping away her tears.

The bus terminal felt cold and lonely, but it had buses leaving for Idaho, which was fortunate. Dani didn't think she could have coped with any further complications. Just leaving Clint was hard enough.

No, she wasn't leaving Clint, she said fiercely. To have left him would have meant that at some point she had truly been with him. And she hadn't. All she had done was live in his house. There was a difference. She had just been fooling herself if she thought otherwise. Time for Mary Sunshine to grow up.

The bus for Idaho wasn't leaving for another hour, the ticket agent told her. Another hour. An hour to sit on a hard bench, thinking hard thoughts. Restlessly, she paced instead.

Two little children raced around her legs, shooting at one another with toy bazookas. The one who had grabbed the back of her leg cried that the other one had no right to shoot him. He was dead!

"Wasn't he dead, lady?" he asked, turning a demanding face up to Dani, his blond hair falling into his eyes as he blinked impatiently.

It seemed so serious to him that she had to smile. "Got you fair and square," she told the other boy, who started to cry and ran off anyway, his brother in hot pursuit. A harried-looking woman caught them both by their arms and dragged them back to their seats.

Dani remembered when she had played games like that with her brother. It had seemed serious then, too, but easily forgotten. Maybe as you grew up the games you played just changed. Maybe love was a game to be quickly forgotten once the score was registered. Didn't the word love mean "nothing" in tennis? Smart people, those tennis players, she thought, sidestepping an empty soda can.

So this is the place where dreams end, she thought as she made a full circle back to her suitcase. In a lonely bus depot heading back home. Well, at least she had a home to go to. Dani lifted the suitcase from the floor, meaning to put it on the seat next to her.

"Just where the hell do you think you're going?"

The suitcase fell from her hands, snapping the feeble lock. Jumbled clothing fell in a disorganized heap on the dirty floor.

"Home," she retorted, snatching up her clothes and dumping them back into the suitcase.

Clint made no effort to help her. Instead he stood towering over her, his hands clenched against his waist. "Just like that?" he demanded.

"No, not 'just like that.' First I have to pack again." She exhaled angrily as she crammed the last of her belongings into the valise. "How did you find me?" San Francisco wasn't American Falls. There had to be several bus terminals in the city, she thought.

"Fred saw you leaving. He followed you and called me on the car phone."

"Good old Fred. Now he can add 'spy' to his list of duties," she said bitterly. "Well, I don't know why you bothered coming down, or is it up?" she asked flippantly. "My sense of direction never was too good," she said, successfully masking the tremor in her voice. "Neither is my timing," she added, her voice momentarily softer as she looked at his face. Then her expression hardened. "But at any rate, you'll be rid of all that shortly. Belle Starr, as you so aptly called me at our first momentous meeting, is going home."

Clint took hold of her shoulders, preventing her flight. He saw the hurt in her eyes and tried to deal with it the best way he could. Having her engagement cancelled like that must have been traumatic for her. Since a career was all she wanted, that had to be what was bothering her. "Harper called and told me what happened."

"I'm sure Barbara will be calling you to explain it all over afternoon tea and seduction," she said sarcastically, trying to shake him loose. The sooner she was out of here, the better, she told herself. She needed time and distance to get her bearings.

He looked at her uncomprehendingly. What was she babbling about? Deciding that her disappointment had temporarily made her take leave of her senses, Clint tried again. "Look, Dani, give me a chance to try to smooth it out. Besides, I—"

But she shook her head. "It's not just that," she insisted, wishing he would let her go. "It's everything."

"What everything?" he asked, trying to keep his voice down. People were beginning to stare. Their behavior was odd, even for a bus terminal in San Francisco.

"I decided I don't like this glitzy world of yours. People stomping over other people as if they were dirt." She pressed her lips together. She might as well tell him all of it. What did she have to lose? "And then there's you," she said darkly.

She felt his hands loosen slightly on her shoulders. "Me?"

"Yes, you. First you blow hot, then cold. First you strip me—" a passing woman gave them both an interested look, then hurried on after receiving a frosty glare from Dani "—of my routine, tell me you're going to make me over, then when I am made over, you act as if you don't like what's there.''

"I—"

"Worse than that, after making me absolutely crazy about you, you act as if I'm a card-carrying, bell-ringing leper. Well, I've had it, do you hear? Had it!" she declared. "You can take it all and stuff it!"

A garbled announcement proclaimed that the bus for Idaho was waiting at gate seven.

"Now if you'll excuse me, that's my bus." Her eyes dared him to stop her.

She saw his jaw harden slightly, the lines in his brow growing deeper as he thought her words over. "All right, Dani, if that's the way you feel."

"That's the way I feel!"

To her utter surprise, he turned and walked away.

She stood there, stunned. He was actually walking away! He wasn't even going to *try* to talk her out of it. She had been right. He was relieved to see her go. She had probably saved him the trouble of telling her that he had made a mistake taking her on. Well, when it came to making mistakes, she had made a beaut! She had given her heart to a cold-blooded, unfeeling man with a handsome face who was no more than an empty shell.

Well, it was over. All over.

Mechanically she turned to walk through the terminal toward her bus. She was worse than a fool for ever allowing herself to get emotionally tied to someone in the business. Jared's leaving had stung her. But this. . . . This was numbing, yet painful beyond belief.

Home was best. Home was safe, she kept telling herself over and over again as she walked. Oh, God, she wasn't going to be able to stand this.

Yes, she could! She had to. There was no other choice.

She wanted to fold up and die.

It took her a moment to find the right bus. She fell in behind a small line of people that were filing by a burly bus driver with a kindly, tired face. Dani held her ticket numbly as she shuffled along in a dreamlike trance. Before she had a chance to present her ticket to the man, he shook his head.

"I'm sorry, you can't get on this bus."

Dani came out of her fog and stared at him. "What?"

"I'm afraid you can't board this bus, miss," he said politely.

People behind her were beginning to grumble. "What's the hold-up, there?" a man barked. He was carrying two suitcases and had a child clinging precariously around his neck.

"Isn't this the right bus?" Dani asked, craning her neck to see the sign over the windshield. She glanced down at her ticket to make sure it matched and that there wasn't some sort of a mix-up. Both were identical. "Look, I don't know what's going on here, but—" she began fiercely. At this point, she was beginning to feel like a cornered dog.

"That's all right, driver; I'll take over from here."

Dani's mouth fell open as Clint walked around the front of the bus. He wore a compassionate smile as he looked down at her. "It's all right, Penelope. I've explained everything."

"What everything?" she cried. "And who's Penelope?" she demanded hotly.

Clint shook his head as he looked at the driver. "These lapses are getting worse and worse," he said.

Through her white-hot anger, she saw nothing but pity in the driver's face.

"Clint, what are you trying to pull?" she cried, utterly confounded. She felt him take a gentle but firm grip on her arm as he began to hustle her aside. With his free hand, he picked up her suitcase.

"Penelope, Mother's worried sick about you. She's run off before," he told the woman behind her, as if in confidence. The dowdy woman nodded knowingly as she clucked in sympathy.

"Clint, so help me . . ." Dani threatened, utterly mortified. Was this his way of getting even with her for running out on him? She was so angry that she was speechless. All she could do was try to pull away from his grasp. She would have had a better chance of growing wings. His hold was relentless.

"The doctor's waiting at the house," he said soothingly. "Just take your medication and everything will be all right again."

Dani pulled back a doubled-up fist and landed it in the pit of his stomach. She succeeded in winning a startled look from Clint and a scraped knuckle where she hit it on his vest button. Rage filled her. Why didn't he just let her go and be done with it? Why was he pulling her back again like a yo-yo.

"Hey, mister, can I hold her for you?" a man at the back of the line offered. It vaguely registered with Dani that the man was apelike and leering.

"No, I can handle her myself," Clint said, as if exercising remarkable patience. With that he lifted her up and slung her over his shoulder, fireman style. With one quick motion he picked up her suitcase again. "Excuse me. Pardon me." He walked nonchalantly through the terminal, as if he didn't have a hundred-and-five-pound ball of fury on his back, pounding angry fists against him.

"I'll scream!" Dani threatened, unable to believe this was happening to her. She managed to grab a terminal guard by the shoulder. "Help, he's kidnapping me!" she cried.

"I see you found her," the guard said to Clint.

Dani slumped against Clint's shoulder, giving up. He had obviously seen to everything, damn him. Thorough. Always thorough.

His progress easier once she had calmed down, Clint hurried to the Mercedes. "I'm going to put you down," he said, digging into his pocket for his keys. "Will you behave?"

"If I don't, are you going to strap me over the hood of your car like a deer?" she asked.

"If that's what it takes to get you home again, yes," he said evenly.

She exhaled loudly. "I'll behave."

"Now you're being sensible," he said, putting her down.

"If I was sensible, I'd be bolting now," she shot back.

He gave her a side glance as he unlocked the car and held the door open for her. "I got my school letter in track."

"Weren't they giving out any for harrassment?" she asked bitingly.

"The school wasn't that progressive," he answered easily, feeling it was best to let her work out her anger verbally.

As if reading his mind and determined to frustrate him, Dani fell into an angry, sullen silence that continued all the way home, despite Clint's efforts at conversation. He carried on as if she were answering him in the appropriate places, the sound of rumbling thunder punctuating his sentences. Finally it began to rain. Huge drops fell against the windshield. The rhythmic swishing of the wipers almost hypnotized her.

"Luckily," he was saying, "Fred got back just in time to see you leave with that battered valise of yours." He glanced at it in the back seat. "We're going to have to get you some better luggage."

"I don't want you to buy me anything else."

"She speaks," he said in feigned surprise as he pulled into the driveway. "It's a miracle!"

"Don't get sarcastic with me," she spat. "I'm the one who has a right to act that way, not you. You just sit back in your plush office and play God."

Clint shook his head. "Knew I should have majored in gibberish. I really could have used it these past few weeks. Want to go in and talk about it?" he asked.

"No," she said crisply, turning her face away. She had already said too much in the terminal. If he didn't understand how she felt—not about her career, but about him—then words weren't going to do any good.

"All right," he said evenly. "Do you want to sit here and talk about it?"

"No!"

"Very well." The next thing she knew, he was pulling her out of the car. Sheets of rain drenched her within the first few seconds. "Then we'll stand out here until you're ready to talk about it, because, damn it, woman, we're going to talk about it *someplace*."

Wind blew her wet hair into her mouth as she opened it to tell him that she thought he was insane. Perversely, she clamped it shut again and glared at him defiantly.

"I knew from the first moment you were different. I

175

didn't realize that meant crazy," he muttered in exasperation as he picked her up again and slung her over his shoulder. Her chin knocked against his back, sinking her teeth into her lower lip, but she refused to cry out.

His key dropped out of his hand as he fumbled with it. Angrily, he banged on the door with his fist. Fred answered almost immediately.

"Will there be two for dinner?" he asked wryly, watching the puddles form on the gleaming tile floor.

Clint didn't bother answering as he stomped up the stairs, a trail of water marking his path. The carpet soaked it up like a blotter and turned a shade darker.

Dani was getting alarmed. How far had she pushed him? What was he planning on doing? She forced herself to be calm. The worst thing she could do would be to show him that she was frightened. She was through trying to emulate the women in his world. If he wanted a fight, he was going to get it!

The only problem was, she thought as he unloaded her abruptly on his bed, she wasn't all that sure what they were fighting about anymore.

"Damn it, why don't you just leave me alone?" she cried. "I have a right to make up my mind about things."

"Don't you think you're overreacting just a little about this morning?" he demanded. "So you lost an engagement. After I talked to Harper, I got you another," he said, pushing her wet hair out of her eyes.

Dani jerked her head back and scrambled off the bed, moving away from him. "I don't *care* about another engagement," she snapped. While the incident had stung her pride and had set her off, it had very little to do with why she had really fled.

"Then what *do* you care about?" he asked, confused. He was giving serious consideration to getting out of the business totally. Ten years was enough time to be around overly emotional, mercurial people. There came a time when you had to think of your own sanity.

"*You,* you big jerk!" she spat out. She saw the look in his eyes turn from wonder to something far, far softer, but when he reached out to touch her, she pulled away. The back of the bed halted her retreat. She made lousy tactical decisions, she thought disparagingly. "I tried to be everything you wanted me to be, and what happened? One moment I had you, the next moment you'd disappear into a mist of work and hurried exits. I was beginning to think I was hallucinating about what was happening between us. What I *thought* was happening between us," she clarified. "Well, I give up," she declared, her blazing eyes forbidding him to touch her. "I can't compete with the likes of Constance Benoit, Barbara Dirken and whoever else you represent."

"Compete?" he echoed.

"Compete," she repeated, annoyed. "As in try to replace. As in jockey for position. I don't know what it would take to make you love me, and it hurts too much to be around you when you don't." She turned her face away from him, her cheeks burning. "I thought that maybe I could do it by being a success, someone for you to be proud of. When Barbara started throwing her weight around, trying to get me fired, it was the last straw. I threw in the towel."

"Dani . . ." His voice was soft, tender, but she still couldn't bring herself to look at him. He would see the hurt in her eyes and probably pity her. She couldn't bear his pity. "I thought you were a fighter."

The hurt abated as she swung around defensively. "I

am a fighter. But only a crazy person keeps walking into haymakers with their chin."

"Haymakers?" he asked.

"Punches," she said. "See, you *don't* know everything," she said, her triumph hollow.

He put his hands on her shoulders, and she felt the warmth flowing into her veins. "I know I want you to come back."

She turned her face up to his, searching for an answer. "Why?"

"Because."

"You're going to have to do better than that," she told him, afraid to believe what she thought she read in his face. "You've got other clients. What do you need from me?"

He stroked her lips lightly with his thumb. "Everything," he breathed against her mouth.

12

Soft kisses covered her lips, growing in intensity, smothering any last protests she might have made and fanning her desire.

Clint pulled her closer, glorying in the pliant way she eagerly molded herself against him.

"You're wet," he murmured against her mouth.

Dani grinned. "I wouldn't throw any rocks if I were you."

"You'd better not keep those clothes on. . . . You'll catch pneumonia."

"What'll I catch if I take them off?" she asked, her eyes sparkling with passion.

"Me." The word was a husky whisper against her throat.

Silently, her eyes never leaving his face, Dani took hold of the sopping hem of her T-shirt.

Clint watched in hushed fascination, feeling his need

for her grow as the T-shirt traveled upward. It slid over the peaks of her breasts, exposing the tiny, straining rose-hued tips beneath the gauzelike bra, and Clint covered them with his hands. As he cupped them gently, his palms began to move slowly, mesmerizingly, evoking a look in her face that was both narcotically hazed and erotically aroused.

"Here," he whispered. "Let me." His hands moved behind her back, undoing the catch of her bra. He kissed every part that was uncovered, coaxing the fabric away with gentle movements.

His kisses trailed along her breasts, then down to her rib cage. Dani closed her eyes, drifting in a sea of ecstasy as she felt the snap of her jeans open. He slowly lowered the zipper, and she shivered uncontrollably. Her need for him grew in intensity as Clint touched her, sliding the jeans down along her hips, her thighs, her calves. He lingered at each point, covering her skin with kisses and caresses that served to drive her wild.

She stepped out of her jeans and was vaguely aware that he cast them aside. Then she became acutely aware of his hands cupping her buttocks, molding her against the hard contours of his firm chest. Caressingly, he removed her panties, then massaged her sweet femininity, producing an agonizing yearning that made her sway involuntarily.

Clint's skin felt as if it were on fire as he absorbed the perfumed essence of her body. Murmuring her name, he caressed the silken core of her femininity with his cheek.

Dani groaned as she felt his tongue do magical things that she had never even considered possible. Her restraint broke as she gave vent to the exquisite agony that was racing through her veins. Her fingers dug into his hair as his tongue penetrated her. She pressed his head against her, murmuring, "Love me."

She thought he whispered back, "I do," but at that moment she couldn't make sense of anything. Fragments of thoughts flashed in and out of her head quickly, leaving behind no recollections. All she could do was feel. She felt the stars, the whirling rainbows, the magic that only he could create for her. She felt the urgent plea of his hardened body.

She was falling, falling, but his arms were there to catch her. Opening her eyes, she realized that he was setting her down on the bed. His own clothes were gone, and she couldn't get enough of the sight of his taut, lean body and the way he so obviously ached for her. In mute supplication, she put her arms out to him.

Clint covered her body with his own, glorying in the ecstasy that was etched on her face. She lifted him higher than he had thought possible with her own ventures to paradise. Seeing and feeling her response excited him further until he transcended his own barriers.

Stroking her, he carried on an intimate exploration until his hands could have reconstructed every curve and valley of her body at will. He felt her sharp intake of breath and the alert posture of her body against him.

"Now, Clint, now," she begged.

He held nothing back.

As he filled her senses and her body, Dani felt a rapturous communion begin that led her to the threshold of heaven and beyond. Their bodies entwined and melded together, creating a whole that had been meant to be since time immemorial, a continuous circle without a beginning or an end.

Finally, an eternity later, she exhaled, utterly spent.

She felt him sag slightly against her. She smiled, enjoying the feel of his body pressing so intimately, so lovingly, against hers. They were together. As they should be.

"Why are you smiling?" he asked, rolling onto his side.

"Just happy," she confessed.

"I can make you even happier."

Her heart pounded. Was he going to ask her to marry him? She knew it was an unrealistic hope. After all, how long had he known her? But she felt as if he had been part of her forever, and she wanted that to continue.

"How?" she asked, taking care to guard herself against disappointment.

He looked mysterious for a moment, unwittingly prolonging her agony. Finally he said, "I have another engagement for you. At the Rainbow Club."

Her eyes grew wide with surprise. "The Rainbow Club?" she echoed, stunned. "I thought only the top names starred there."

"They do. But we're not talking about starring. We're talking about being an opening act."

She frowned slightly. "Like with Barbara?"

"No, not like with Barbara," he said, playing with a strand of her hair. Pure gold. Pure, just like she was. He felt his desire begin to rise again. Would he ever get his fill of her? He doubted it. The thought made him happy. But she was waiting to hear about the engagement, so he went on talking business, even though he wanted to crush her mouth against his again. "This time, you'll be opening for Ella Jackson. Ella *has* no ego problem. It's a wonderful start," he told her.

That it was. She raised herself up on her elbow. Her

hair had already dried, and now it spread over her shoulder like a gossamer veil. Clint brought a strand of it to his lips as she talked. "How did you manage that?" she asked.

"Played your tape for the owner. He likes your style," he said simply.

"And you?" she whispered, her full lips a scant inch away from his.

He threw her back down on the pillow, cradling her against his body.

"I thought I already made my point. Guess I'll have to show you all over again."

"Show me," she coaxed huskily. "Show me."

The rest of the afternoon dissolved into a haze of lovemaking that left them both tired and deliciously content.

The fury of the storm had passed, and Dani listened sleepily to the sound of the rain rhythmically falling against the bedroom window. Clint lay next to her, holding her tightly even in his sleep. She liked the secure feeling his gesture evoked. She liked belonging to him. Carefully, she raised her head and kissed his cheek.

His hold tightened. "You're going to have to do better than that."

She laughed. "I didn't know you were awake." She leaned her arm against his chest and looked into his eyes, trying to decide what it was about him that she loved best.

"Trying to ravage me in my sleep?"

"Something like that." She lowered her mouth to his.

Clint threaded his fingers through her tousled hair,

cupping the back of her head and holding her to him as he kissed her back. "Ready for more?" he asked mischievously.

The twinkle in her eyes matched his own. "Always."

He watched the earrings he had given her swing as she tossed her head gaily. He touched one, running his finger lightly along the ivory characters, trailing a path down the side of her neck that made her shiver with anticipation.

"They mean I love you."

She stared at him. "What?"

"The earrings. I said I'd tell you when the time came. It's come," he said quietly. "I love you."

"Oh, Clint." Tears sprang to her eyes and quickly spilled out.

He rubbed them aside with his thumb, amazed. "Why are you crying?"

"Because I'm so happy."

"Women . . ." He shook his head, pretending confusion.

"When?"

"When what?" Now *he* was confused.

"When did you know that you loved me?" she pressed eagerly. Teasingly, she began to drop light, fleeting kisses on his chest.

Desire clouded his thoughts. How he wanted her. "Since the night you came to me wearing that aqua cloud—Dani, if you expect me to try to make any sense, you're going to have to stop doing that." He put his hands on her shoulders and drew her up to him, looking into her face. His expression grew serious. "When Fred told me that you'd run off, I realized that I'd rather be with you, no matter what you were like, than without you."

Dani felt a bitter pang. "Then it does bother you," she whispered sadly. "My being unsophisticated."

He looked at her, thunderstruck. "It bothers me when you *are* sophisticated. When you began acting differently I was afraid. . . ."

"What?" This mystery between them had to be unraveled. She had to know what he wanted from her.

"That in time you'd be like all the others, that you'd lose that wonderful naive look I love, that bright, vibrant way of looking at things."

She nodded her head, finally understanding. "You were afraid," she said slowly, "that I was going to turn into a self-centered, grasping woman. That I wanted to use you."

He nodded.

Dani rose to her knees, unmindful that the sheet fell away and left her utterly naked before him. Her hands were on her hips, her expression hurt. "Do you think that little of me?" she demanded. "That I could turn into a conceited barracuda just because of a little success? I was just trying to act more like what you were used to. I thought that if I were more sophisticated, more worldly, I'd stand a better chance against the Barbaras in your life."

"There never *were* any Barbaras in my life, only in my career," he told her, his eyes devouring her.

"Well," she said, her anger disappearing as quickly as it had flared, "no matter what sort of clothes you're going to put on me, I'm going to be Dani Christopher."

He pulled her down to him, unable to restrain himself any longer. "No, you're not."

"I'm not?" she echoed dumbly. "You're going to change my name as well as my clothes and my routine?"

"Something like that. I'm old-fashioned enough to think that Mr. and Mrs. MacPherson would look better on our stationery than Clint MacPherson and Dani Christopher."

It took a minute for the words to sink in. "Are you asking me to marry you?" she gasped at last.

"I'm not doing a very good job, but yes, that's the gist of it. I can get you a long-playing engagement as Dani MacPherson."

She curled up against his chest. "What's the pay like?"

"Barter system," he answered. "Everything you give, you get back in kind."

"Sounds good to me." She paused for a moment, her mouth hovering over his. She could see the unbridled passion in his eyes. She had him, she thought joyfully. He was as trapped as she was. "Clint?"

"Yes?"

"Make sure that the contract is ironclad."

"I will," he promised. "I will." He folded his arms around her and loved her with every fiber of his being. This time, the world disappeared for them both.

ENTER:

Here's your chance to win a fabulous $50,000 diamond jewelry collection, consisting of diamond necklace, bracelet, earrings and ring.

All you have to do to enter is fill out the coupon below and mail it by September 30, 1985.

Send entries to:

In the U.S.	Silhouette Diamond Sweepstakes P.O. Box 779 Madison Square Station New York, NY 10159
In Canada	Silhouette Diamond Sweepstakes Suite 191 238 Davenport Road Toronto, Ontario M5R 1J6

NAME_____

ADDRESS_____

CITY_____ STATE/(PROV.)_____

ZIP/(POSTAL CODE)_____

BCD-A-1

RULES FOR SILHOUETTE DIAMOND SWEEPSTAKES

OFFICIAL RULES—NO PURCHASE NECESSARY

1. Silhouette Diamond Sweepstakes is open to Canadian (except Quebec) and United States residents 18 years or older at the time of entry. Employees and immediate families of the publishers of Silhouette, their affiliates, retailers, distributors, printers, agencies and RONALD SMILEY INC. are excluded.

2. To enter, print your name and address on the official entry form or on a 3″ x 5″ slip of paper. You may enter as often as you choose, but each envelope must contain only one entry. Mail entries first class in Canada to Silhouette Diamond Sweepstakes, Suite 191, 238 Davenport Road, Toronto, Ontario M5R 1J6. In the United States, mail to Silhouette Diamond Sweepstakes, P.O. Box 779, Madison Square Station, New York, NY 10159. Entries must be postmarked between February 1 and September 30, 1985. Silhouette is not responsible for lost, late or misdirected mail.

3. First Prize of diamond jewelry, consisting of a necklace, ring, bracelet and earrings will be awarded. Approximate retail value is $50,000 U.S./$62,500 Canadian. Second Prize of 100 Silhouette Home Reader Service Subscriptions will be awarded. Approximate retail value of each is $162.00 U.S./$180.00 Canadian. No substitution, duplication, cash redemption or transfer of prizes will be permitted. Odds of winning depend upon the number of valid entries received. One prize to a family or household. Income taxes, other taxes and insurance on First Prize are the sole responsibility of the winners.

4. Winners will be selected under the supervision of RONALD SMILEY INC., an independent judging organization whose decisions are final, by random drawings from valid entries postmarked by September 30, 1985, and received no later than October 7, 1985. Entry in this sweepstakes indicates your awareness of the Official Rules. Winners who are residents of Canada must answer correctly a time-related arithmetical skill-testing question to qualify. First Prize winner will be notified by certified mail and must submit an Affidavit of Compliance within 10 days of notification. Returned Affidavits or prizes that are refused or undeliverable will result in alternative names being randomly drawn. Winners may be asked for use of their name and photo at no additional compensation.

5. For a First Prize winner list, send a stamped self-addressed envelope postmarked by September 30, 1985. In Canada, mail to Silhouette Diamond Contest Winner, Suite 309, 238 Davenport Road, Toronto, Ontario M5R 1J6. In the United States, mail to Silhouette Diamond Contest Winner, P.O. Box 182, Bowling Green Station, New York, NY 10274. This offer will appear in Silhouette publications and at participating retailers. Offer void in Quebec and subject to all Federal, Provincial, State and Municipal laws and regulations and wherever prohibited or restricted by law.

Genuine Silhouette sterling silver bookmark for only $15.95!

What a beautiful way to hold your place in your current romance! This genuine sterling silver bookmark, with the distinctive Silhouette symbol in elegant black, measures 1½″ long and 1″ wide. It makes a beautiful gift for yourself, and for every romantic you know! And, at only $15.95 each, including all postage and handling charges, you'll want to order several now, while supplies last.

Send your name and address with check or money order for $15.95 per bookmark ordered to
Simon & Schuster Enterprises
120 Brighton Rd., P.O. Box 5020
Clifton, N.J. 07012
Attn: Bookmark

Bookmarks can be ordered pre-paid only. No charges will be accepted. Please allow 4-6 weeks for delivery.

She fought for a bold future
until she could no longer
ignore the...

ECHO OF THUNDER

MAURA SEGER

Author of Eye of the Storm

ECHO OF THUNDER is the love story of James
Callahan and Alexis Brockton, who forge a union
that must withstand the pressures of their own
desires and the challenge of building a new television
empire.

Author Maura Seger's writing has been described by
Romantic Times as having a "superb blend of
historical perspective, exciting romance and a deep
and abiding passion for the human soul."

**Available at your favorite
retail outlet in SEPTEMBER.**

ECO-B-1

Silhouette Desire

COMING NEXT MONTH

BEYOND LOVE—Ann Major
Nine years had passed since a misunderstanding had
forced Dinah to leave Morgan Hastings. Armed with the
truth, Morgan set out to win her back.

THE TENDER STRANGER—Diana Palmer
After a whirlwind romance, Dani St. Clair found herself
blissfully married to a man she hardly knew. Nothing could
have shattered her happiness...until his dangerous secret was
revealed.

MOON MADNESS—Freda Vasilos
Two years of separation had changed nothing. Jason
Stephanou was still the only man capable of driving all reason
from Sophie's mind. He was the one she loved. How could she
leave him again?

STARLIGHT—Penelope Wisdom
An accident suddenly ended jockey Trevor Laird's career and
brought her face-to-face once again with Steven Montford, the
man she had always loved, and the father of a child he didn't
know existed.

YEAR OF THE POET—Ann Hurley
Child psychologist Joyce Lanier had a good head on her
shoulders. Little could rattle this calm professional until wild
Irish poet Neill Riorden pierced her reserve and shook her to
her very core.

A BIRD IN HAND—Dixie Browning
When Anny Cousins decided to take in a boarder from the
nearby university, she looked forward to playing dominoes
with a stodgy old professor. She was in for a big surprise!

AVAILABLE THIS MONTH

SIMPLE PLEASURES
Lynda Trent

COUNTRY BLUE
Marie Nicole

NO SENSE OF HUMOR
Elizabeth Alden

ANNA'S CHILD
Angel Milan

ALL THE MARBLES
Beverly Bird

RAND EMORY'S WOMAN
Nicole Monet